RETURN OF THE

HORLA

Other Titles in the Adam Quatrology

RETURN OF THE

A NOVEL

BERNARD SUSSMAN

Bartleby Press
Washington • Baltimore

Cover illustration and design by Ralph Butler

ISBN 978-0935437-53-9
Library of Congress Control Number: 2011940644

Published by:

Bartleby Press

PO Box 858
Savage, Maryland 20763
800-953-9929
www.BartlebythePublisher.com

Printed in the United States of America

For Callum

One

Doctor Rogoff's waiting room was no better than ten years before. It was comfortable enough, but remained a dreary place. And much like Adam himself, it had not worn well over the intervening years, becoming in fact, quite tacky. Nor did it help much that another patient, sitting across from him, a guy he couldn't quite place, looked nevertheless, somewhat familiar. Unreasonable to hope that this other man eyes averted or no, had not spotted him as well. So much for getting oneself discretely repsychoanalized at Doctor Rogoff's.

But maybe it wouldn't come to that. He'd heard that nowadays there were all kinds of new drugs for just about every kind of mental disorder. His new condition could possibly be dispensed with expeditiously, biochemically, and he wouldn't have to deal with the prospective embarrassment of running into other Washington familiars week after conceivably endless weeks in this oppressive antechamber from out of which two or three psychiatrists other than his own Rogoff fished their flaky catches, ushering them

1

into adjacent consulting rooms so as to either manipulate them or convince them of something or other.

A new condition? Was he really feeling different from that other time? Was he not every bit as anxious as he'd been back then? Well... anxious, yes. But it wasn't the same. Because now it was something else, something entirely unexpected. After all the years of assuming it was finished and done with, he'd been taken over once again by the same old evil one. This present anxiety wasn't about too much alcohol, or women, or guilt. It was about his Horla. The Horla, incredibly back again, after leaving him alone for thirty odd years and allowing him not a moment's peace.

"Adam. Good to see you. Come on in."

Rogoff, now gray-bearded and no longer fastening his collar, or for that matter even bothering to draw up his tie, had revealed himself. He stood before the open doorway to his consulting chamber, looking affable enough, yet intent.

Adam, without saying a single word to his doctor, merely rose with a nod and was directed inside, where Rogoff pointed him towards the familiar old leather chair. It now showed further signs of hard wear with more than a few new coffee stains and several burn holes from cigarettes Adam didn't remember.

Doctor Rogoff, except for the raggedly trimmed beard, looked and sounded much the same. But his consulting room, a privileged and spacious chamber with ornate fireplace befitting his professional seniority, appeared to have been kept up no better than the run-down gathering place outside. Its oriental carpet had become quite threadbare in places and previously gaping cracks in the leather cushion of his own armchair had become so widened that its interior felt padding protruded outward through them as soon as he got seated.

Adam was addressed a second time. "Make yourself comfortable, Adam."

However seedy his surroundings, the old boy still remained his grandly commanding self.

"Well then. What's up?"

"Is that how we begin, nowadays? With a `What's up?'"

"Come on now, Adam. Let's not waste time with any of your old picayune compulsive crap. For God's sake, get to it. Let me in on whatever's eating you now. And Christ. Don't get any idea we are `beginning' anything. I have attained the ripe old age of seventy-eight and have no intention of ever again putting in three hours a week, and maybe years and years, with the likes of someone like you."

"You still consider me your very worst patient?"

"Well if not the absolute worst, you've always been right up there."

"Thank you very much. And what do you mean by `compulsive'? You never told me I was compulsive."

"What in God's name would you call this? When... let me in on it, would you? Can I hope to get you started? What will we have to go through before I get the semblance of a straightforward answer to a simple question like, `How are you'?"

"That's not exactly how you put it. You said `What's up?'"

"Okay. How are you?"

"You still getting ninety-five an hour?"

"Don't change the subject. I said `How are you?'. Damn it. So answer the question. And ninety-five is not what I charge for something like this. For this, from you, I want one-fifty."

"Terrible. I feel absolutely terrible. Did you save your old notes?"

"What notes?"

"The ones you used to scribble. You know. In that ratty old spiral notebook of yours while I ventilated and just about spilled my guts out. Over there on that lumpy old couch of yours. Hey man. Where'd it go to? Damned if that smelly old thing isn't gone."

"I got rid of it. We do things differently nowadays. We're much less analytical. More direct...supportive. And sometimes, pharmacological."

"And maybe more sanitary, I should hope. But you kept your notes, right?"

"They're probably around here somewhere. Why?"

"Well...you remember the Horla?"

"The what?"

"Son-of-a-bitch. How could you possibly forget something like that? Check your notes, man. Or were you writing letters to your kids or maybe just doodling back there, once you got settled in and feelin' comfy? Or even grabbin' quick naps? You wanta know somethin'? There were times I suspected as much. After all, you had me damned well blindsided. And anyway, how could I know if you were actually payin' any attention to what I was sayin'? I was doin' all the talkin. Hardly ever was there so much as a peep out of you."

"It is now two hundred dollars an hour and going up."

Undeterred by that prospect, Adam flashed his revelation.

"The Horla? The Horla is what had me between nine

and thirteen. Just like in the story by de Maupassant. He'd get on to me, all of a sudden, every so often, and have me feeling like I was gonna faint. Like I was sinking, slipping away, maybe even dying. And he'd also make me do things, all sorts of things, over, and over, and over again."

"Like I said. You were compulsive and obsessive regarding much of what you did. But I don't remember any claim of your being under the influence of something supernatural. How would you spell that?"

"Horla. H-O-R-L-A. And I'll say it again. Not once did you ever make a diagnosis of me bein' obsessive-compulsive. Christ. If that's what you were thinkin', I sure as hell had a right to know about it. Tell me this. Couldn't you get yourself sued for something like that? Isn't there some kinda right and standard way for psychiatrists to conduct themselves so people like me are protected against that kind of a screw-up?"

"No there isn't. We are not into cookbook psychiatry, yet. Or cookbook medicine either, for that matter. We physicians have considerable clinical leeway, thank God. It's called professional discretion. But it's sure wonderful having you back, Adam. I'd almost forgotten how lively you used to make it around here. Now ... is there anything I can do for you aside from rummaging through my old files and searching for your god-damned Horla?"

"It seems to me you never believed in God. The way I remember it you always said it was unnecessary. You even called it totally incomprehensible, how any one could go for something that foolish. And yet, this is the fifth time you've called on Him since I'm in here. Do you realize that?"

"What I'm realizing is that I couldn't possibly be

needed for something like this. So how about letting me off the hook? I'll just go and settle down in one of the other consulting rooms with a real patient. You know. Like someone who's here to talk about their concerns and wanting to be helped. And if you like, you can stay right where you are for the balance of the session. You can even make believe I'm still here and jabber your fool head off to your heart's content."

"If you absolutely must take a leak, go right ahead. Otherwise, don't make a move until I've had my hour's worth."

"These days I'm only doing forty-five minute sessions. Thank God."

"There. You did it again. When did you get yourself converted? Seems like every other word out of you is `God'."

"Look Adam. Nine years ago, in a certain way I thought I'd been delivered when you stopped coming by to see me. But now it looks like I need to be delivered again. And I'm open to any help I can get. From whatever quarter I can devise."

Minutes passed in silence, neither one of them conceding the other more than a glance. Adam started it up again, almost angrily.

"I have to do everything a dozen times. It's just like when I was ten years old."

"That's called checking. You've always had a bit of it. And no matter what I used to say concerning your tendency in that direction, you'd insist invariably on writing it off as part of your inclination to be careful, even meticulous, in everything you did."

"Yeah. Yeah. Now I remember. You handed me that

cock-and-bull line about it being my way to save myself from dying. By getting everything just right, you know... perfect, I was thinking, but all the same subconsciously, that I could hang on just about forever. What a crock! Look, none of this stuff is about me being a perfectionist. It's about me going fucking well nuts. I am staring at my garage door, looking at it over and over again, with no let-up, just to be sure I've really run the fucker down. I am turning off the stove, twenty, thirty, times. Man! One of these days I'm gonna bust a knob off'a the damned thing. And in spite of all this shit I am spending more than an hour every night trying to convince myself that, finally, I've really got the place locked up good enough so I can head upstairs and hit the sack. That damned Horla is back here again after all these years, and with a vengeance. You got any ideas as to how we handle this situation or do I go and get myself one of them exorcists?"

"You still in politics?"

"Sure. I just signed up a couple of newly elected damned- fool congressmen. And they're doin' exactly as I tell them. Although my main hustle, like always...if you remember, is fund raising. But what's that got to do with any of what I'm telling you?"

"It's just that obsessive-compulsives seem to get worse, or have flare ups, following life style changes or set backs at work. That's what may have happened to you the last time. And listening to you now, I've been wondering if this was just more of the same."

"You sure you remember my case? The way I recall it, Herr Doctor, my old problem was not about being obsessive-compulsive. It was all about too much booze, too many women, not a helluva lot of sleep, and an evaporating bank account, mixed with a good enough dose of anxiety and guilt over my wife maybe finding out. If `checking' is your word for what I'm doing this time, the only thing I ever `checked' out back then was whatever good looking chick happened to be coming my way, and how to hang out with her without being nailed either by the wife, or anyone else who might recognize me. I grant you, like with everything else I've ever been into, I was pulling it off just about perfectly, but ultimately at one hell of a price. Somehow the wife found out anyway. Next thing I know she's dumping me and taking me to the cleaners. So one fine day right after that, I just straight out got my act together, stopped acting so fucking self destructive, and quit coming in here to see you. But never, never, not even once, did you make me out for some kind of a big time obsessive-compulsive freak."

"You simply repressed what I was telling you. At the time it wasn't the main problem for you anyway...that is, emotionally. Besides which, back then your compulsive tendency was easy enough for you to cope with. Now, and for some reason we may or may not ever be able to identify, that particular behavioral inclination has simply recurred and gotten a bit worse."

"Simply? I just love the way you see things. Look man. My brain has been invaded by the Horla. It has taken over my mind. It is jerking my chain, pulling all the strings. It is in control of my every thought, my every move."

"Look. Use your head, Adam. Don't go bonkers over some silly French ghost story you read a million years ago when you were a naive and impressionable kid. What you've described to me is a well known clinical syndrome. And nowadays much more is understood about it than even a couple of years ago. Today, we have several effective treatments for obsessive-compulsive disorder. By combining drugs and behavioral therapy it's possible to obtain a better than sixty per cent improvement rate. And we no longer approach it as a psychodynamic problem. It's all about neurotransmitters in the brain and anatomical deviations from normal. In fact, with certain kinds of x-rays or scans, we can actually detect physical changes in the brains of such patients."

"You mean you can take a picture of the inside of my head and see the Horla? Well zap him on out of there. And I want the fucker one hundred per cent gone. Sixty percent is for the birds."

"Adam, I hate to say it, but you are an even worse listener now than you were nine years ago. The way this sort of thing still goes, if there's to be any chance at all for it to work, is that you describe your symptoms. Then, you listen very carefully while I try and come up with solutions. But the way I'm seeing it, based upon your present attitude, you might just as well head right on out of here and either find yourself that exorcist or simply do your own zapping. Meaning you could go and shoot yourself in the head. And if you should opt for the second course, thinking you can nail your damned Horla but miss your brain, then you are even crazier than I have ever given you credit for."

"Look. Let's just say I'm not exactly enthralled with the odds you're offering. That's because I'm really in a worse way than maybe you appreciate. For instance. All I have to do is dial a telephone number and that same stupid number keeps repeating and repeating in my head until I get to dial some other number or do something, anything, involving numbers. Right now it's eleven o'clock, right? It took me quite a while to walk over here from my office. Let's say maybe twenty minutes. But you wanta hear something pathetic? All the time I'm walkin' over here, the last number I dialed before I left the office is repeatin', goin' round and round in my head without a moment's let-up. It's fucking horrible. And even worse than that. Sometimes out of nowhere, absolutely nowhere, there are numbers poppin' up in my brain I can't even account for. So if your saying, assuming I get drugged up to your satisfaction, that all I'll really have to deal with is forty percent of this crap, then I'm a goner anyway, a sure-fire goner. And the decent thing for you to do is find some legitimate way to put me out of my misery."

"Are you feeling depressed?"

"Is that supposed to be a serious question? Where in hell you comin' from, doc? In my situation, who wouldn't be? Of course I'm depressed. All I think about is how the Horla had that guy at the end of the story. The poor bastard couldn't take it any more and decided to knock himself off. How he did it was never quite spelled out. But even so, the other weird thing is I'm dead certain, anyway, that he hung himself in his own clothes closet. Man. I can even see him hanging there."

Rogoff chose to ignore that little bit of coloration.

"The only reason I asked about depression is I think you ought to be aware of the fact that the drugs we use for this condition are all strong antidepressants. They'll probably give you a lift."

"Great. I can enjoy bein' miserable. Right, doc? Listen. Tell me this. Think any of the other shrinks around here might just happen to have a better handle on all of this?

Today, I've got time to burn anyway. Should I just head back on out and sit in the waiting room? Maybe one of the younger hot shots workin' out of this place knows something you're not on to. How about it? Want to set it up for me?"

"Being negative, Adam, is not the answer. What's wrong with simply starting treatment and seeing what comes of it? Who knows? You might do better than the published claims."

"What's the downside? The side effects? This isn't like that toxic psychiatry one of your buddies down the block is always screaming about on TV, is it?"

"Some patients feel keyed up. They call it being wired. Otherwise, maybe there'd be a little nausea, or headache, or dizziness, but nothing that ordinarily lasts. If you get jittery or have trouble sleeping, I can always give you something to combat that. The drug I've been using for obsessive-compulsive disorder is Prozac. We start with a low dose and then gradually increase it. And at the same time you'll be coached in what we call the behavioral approach. I can refer you to someone who specializes in that sort of thing."

"How do you go about that?"

"Well first off, a therapist goes with you to where you do most of your checking and encourages you not to do it. If with that kind of support you are able to resist performing the compulsive act, then after awhile you may be able to hold off on your own. That's it in a nutshell."

"You hit on exactly the right word for it. It's nutty. God damned nutty as hell. Just say `no', right?"

"Adam. If you insist on being negative, we will get nowhere."

"Any of these so called therapists young and good looking?"

"I'll see what I can do. Didn't you just get finished saying you were cured of all of that?"

"Look. Maybe if you team me up with someone who says nothing but `yes', I'll be able to make with a `no'. You know, get myself kind of inspired. Just a suggestion, that's all."

"All right then. Any real questions?"

"None I can think of right now."

"Okay then. I'm writing you a prescription and I'll see you in a week. If you call back, the secretary will have the name and number of a behavioral therapist."

"Look. If this doesn't work out, how about one of those new laser treatments? I hear they're terrific."

"I'm not sure how that's relevant to what we've been talking about."

"Well, the way I understand it is that a laser ray can destroy tissue just about anywhere, even in your eye, and without hittin' anything else that happens to be close by. So instead, like you said, of me in some kind of desperation shooting myself in the head and eliminating once and for all, not only the Horla but myself as well, all kidding aside, what's so unreasonable about zapping the Horla real selective like, with the laser?"

"A regular gun would be much more preferable. Get on out of here, Adam. Just start the medicine. Take two a day."

Two

Anew group of aspiring escapees from the heights of despair had arranged themselves in the waiting room. Adam, outbound now, and sighting no other Washington familiars, considered himself fortunate to avoid further exposure. But why was it that only in this sort of waiting room people seemed so fixed upon sneaking stares at one another? Clearly, there existed much more curiosity regarding the next person's mental equilibrium than what might be their intestinal fortitude. Such incursive inquisitiveness and the touchy risk of some kind of personal boundary violation could be very trying to a guarded fellow like Adam.

He hurriedly retrieved his coat and made a quick exit, eager to head for the nearest pharmacy and avoid any more of this sick and snoopy eye-balling. The closest one happened to be right across the street. But once downstairs he was plagued by a bothersome inclination to retrace his steps, even at the risk of encountering that same nosy bunch back in the waiting room, in order to quiz his psychiatrist a bit further. Something still needed flushing out, some kind of vague, unresolved, business. But nothing surfaced or could be forced to mind. So resisting the urge to retrace his steps he stayed the course for the pharmacy.

He attributed this oddity to a familiarly irksome sense of noncompletion, an abiding feeling he'd had for weeks now of nothing, absolutely nothing, ever being quite over and done with, that is, finished and brought to some kind, to any kind, of acceptibly conclusive, and recognizably verifiable end point, when to every reasonable appearance, and the evidence afforded by the usual senses that most people bring to bear upon such determinations, it was very much and quite obviously the case.

But then he wondered, might this not be the Horla's central strategy for taking him over, the ingenious trick at the heart of the evil one's agenda? And if that were the situation, it was hard to imagine how Rogoff's puny little pills could take on an adversary of such formidable wile.

But hadn't De Maupassant's fellow considered giving poison pills to his Horla? As it turned out, fearing discovery, his man had given up on that idea. And instead, believing the Horla right there beside him, he'd locked up, ducked outside, and set his place on fire. Unfortunately the poor guy incinerated his servants as well as the house. But not the Horla. Well, these were different times, different pills, and trickier methods. Perhaps with Rogoff's more sophisticated connivance he'd nail the Horla once and for all. At least, it was worth a try.

After a single inquiring glance from the pharmacist, Adam was ready to bolt. He felt certain that this little owl-faced fellow, having squinted at Rogoff's prescription, was sizing him up, and deciding which in particular of the common types of weirdo stood before his counter out of pressing need for the presumably potent, psychotropic brainbuster Rogoff had ordered up for him. It was like being back in the waiting room all over again, but much worse, because here was someone who didn't have to look him over and guess. Here was someone who truly had his number.

Adam's apprehension stemmed from the fact that he had always put considerable effort into craftily cloaking his day-to-day professional operations. It was how he'd managed to stay in demand as a political consultant and the same modus operandi had been carried over into his personal life. But now, by a quick and just about casual twirl of Rogoff's pen across the face of an indifferent, yet all too incriminating prescription pad, Adam, to his impending mortification, risked indelible branding as one of variously described kinds of deranged nut.

After all, during the previous treatment under Rogoff there'd only been talk therapy. Confidential talk therapy. And should any of that ever come to light, he could easily pass it off as what lots of people, even big time creative oddballs, might commonly do, as a way of tapping into unrealized or latent talent. Psychoanalysis had had its run as a popular "in thing" and for some few it was still very much in vogue. Once in awhile one might even hear envy expressed for those fortunate enough to carry the stiff tab for all of their long years of presumed "self-actualization". So on that score he'd never had any real concerns.

But this was another thing entirely. This was about getting into drugs: anti-depressants, uppers, downers, and who knew what else before he'd finally be done with them? And meanwhile he'd be running the risk of getting found out and nailed as one of those drug dependent notables the news hounds just loved to uncover. Adam could read the terrible consequences of what Rogoff was doing to him as they registered upon the prissy little druggist's all too knowing face.

Although the man's query was straightforward enough, what he was really thinking had to be something else.

"You'll be waiting on this?"

"How long's it gonna take?"

"Maybe ten minutes or so. I hope to tell you though, your doctor's put you on one helluva drug. And real popular too. These days, it seems like just about everybody walkin' in here's either on it or tried it, at least once. Anyway, look here...why don't you just head on over there, grab yourself a seat and take the time to read over the instructions. I'll have it for you in a jiffy."

"Sounds good to me."

Adam thought he might have judged the man too hastily. After all, rather than looking askance, the little guy had kind of welcomed him into a pharmaceutical drug fest of sorts.

Reading from the little sheet of paper handed him by the pharmacist he grasped immediately that what he'd been given was an edited computer printout commonly supplied to patients regarding proper dosage for prescription drugs and what to look out for in the event of possibly adverse side effects. Well now! This Prozac had better be worth the taking because here was stuff that went far beyond anything Rogoff had intimated could happen. Unless all of this was so much self protective pharmacological boiler plate, it appeared that even one or two doses of Prozac were quite capable of bringing on what would definitely not be a win-win situation. Heart attack, allergic shock, stroke, high blood pressure, convulsions, tremors, and almost every other kind of heavy way to depart this world, were set forth in alarming detail. Christ, this designer drug, something called a serotonin uptake inhibitor, had big time muscle. Well then. Maybe...just maybe...it could truly happen. Prozac might pack enough of a wallop to put his damned Horla right out of business.

As soon as the pharmacist passed it across the counter, Adam took off, having secured his small bottle of Prozac capsules to an inside pocket of his jacket.

On a Friday mid-afternoon he'd usually have to catch up on his telephone messages. With that in mind he headed for his I Street office but paused along the way just long enough to reach for a single, twenty milligram, green and yellow capsule. Hesitating for a moment, but then hoping for the best, he gulped it down. Although Rogoff had warned him not to anticipate anything dramatic happening over the short run, and had insisted there'd be little, if any, benefit for at least two weeks, Adam stopped again about half-way along his route to take stock of himself. He couldn't be too careful with something like this. Especially since he'd had no previous experience with powerful medications.

Nothing. He felt nothing at all. Well, he realized, at least he wasn't verging on some kind of quick, major allergic reaction. But what about those other drug warnings? He'd better pay close attention. No point in running unecessary risks.

It would take him at least another ten minutes to reach the I Street office but oddly enough, certain benches inside the little park at Dupont Circle were drawing his attention as he started to pass them by. This was a familiar route and the thought of lingering there had never occurred to him. In fact, Adam had not been one to ever sit on a park bench, anywhere, much less those at Dupont Circle where the most peculiar kinds of people were apt to hang out. Besides, he'd always been much too busy, or fidgety, for something that leisurely. So it was a strange move on his part when he found himself doing just that, but it was not to be avoided.

He'd gotten himself seated. And because? Well because... wasn't it a sunny spring day turned somehow gloriously warm? And didn't a closefelt soft breeze seem to harbor all kinds of marvelous scents? Were not young buds erupting just about everywhere? And could he not anticipate the newly sprouted tendrils of bright green vine starting to snake their way from out their dark hiding places amongst the shadows? There was a sense of time suddenly suspended and turned quite heady. Heaven itself was smiling, smiling down upon him, upon him alone. And beaming, beaming as heaven most surely beams, under the absolute requirement of having to do none other. Why, this park could pass for heaven itself. Or for being pervaded by so much beauty, a sign, at least, of heaven's existence above or about there somewhere.

The strangeness proceeded to intensify. Not only was everything about him dazzling, but benevolently uplifting as well, because aside from the ethereal warmth, it seemed that there was a supportive, friendly presence hovering this gleaming, shimmering, all-out fired up pleasantry. And it was hovering Dupont Circle so splendiferously that the neighboring streets leading into Dupont Circle by way of

Connecticut and Massachusetts Avenues were becoming in-
fused with some quite astounding flashes and scintillations.
What a fantastic thing to experience! His run-of-the-mill,
workaday, political base was being transformed, just like
that, into an extravagantly upbeat spectacle.

Then, just as quickly... a fucking black hole. It all re-
verted to mundane, tedious reality. Why, this entire damned
thing was for the birds. Pigeons, in fact, and they were
crapping all around him. But never mind some spooky
kind of heaven turned suddenly sour. What sort of hoax,
right here, in what was nothing more than a corner of hell,
had been worked upon him? It was the Prozac. It just had
to be the Prozac.

But Prozac wasn't supposed to come into its own and
take charge of things for at least another two weeks. And
neither Rogoff nor the druggist's printout had suggested
anything about such obviously inappropriate sensations of
well-being, or of getting off on some kind of cosmic high.
Clearly, he'd been deprived of full medical advisement
regarding this drug and maybe duped as well.

He felt put upon, and with nowhere else to fix the
blame, he had half a mind to double back to Rogoff and
charge the son-of-a-bitch with medical negligence. Until,
realizing that the strange vibrations, both good and bad,
had finally backed off entirely, rather than staying pissed
off at Rogoff, he became resentful of somehow losing out.
After all, good feelings of any kind were hard to come
by these days, and he hadn't a clue to any conceivable
formula for regenerating them other than popping down
more of these pills. But the prospect of needing to do
something like that, especially on a regular basis, had him
more depressed than ever.

"Hey man. Awesome. Ain't it?"

A young man had materialized right beside him on the bench. Adam eyed him with distaste. He had no interest whatever in anything this guy might be jabbering about, nor in being drawn into a banal exchange of pleasantries. He shot back, reflexively.

"No."

"No? No? Why look at how all them people are carryin' on, each a' them bein' into somethin' different. Awesome is how I see it. And you say `No'?"

This young squirt, so free with his kudos, just begged a put-down. Adam was quick to oblige.

"Christ. Is that what you call placing one foot in front of another? My take on it is they're a bunch of simple-minded idiots. Look at them. No sooner do they shut their mouths, than they crack them open. And once they're wide open, they clam up again. All I'm seein' is a bunch of damned fools with fixed ways of doin' things over and over they couldn't shake off if they tried. Chances are it started even before they learned to walk."

"You some kinda psychologist?"

His uninvited inquisitor was the usual scruffy, unshaven, kind of Dupont hanger-on, with hair ponytailing down his backside, and legs bared beyond the raggedy edges of well worn denim shorts. He was footed out in cracked leather sandals the soles of which were starting to come apart. Although he didn't smell too badly, Adam, ever the tidy one, caught enough of a whiff to shift his position.

"No."

"That all you ever have to say? Again with the `no'?"

Adam opted for haughty but erudite. "It was a perfectly adequate answer to a very simple question but if you insist on being further enlightened, one doesn't have to be a psychologist to appreciate that in many ways we're all little more than dumb robots. And every so often our circuitry goes haywire. That's when we start hittin' the bottle, fuckin' our brains out, gorgin' everlastingly, or gettin' hooked on doin' certain dumb and self-destructive things over and over again, until finally they wind up circlin' 'round and 'round and knockin' us off. And then there are those who go completely looney. The ones who just hang out spendin' all their time checkin', and verifyin', every last bit of all the shitty and ordinary everyday stuff they're into, makin' sure each and every damned fool thing that needs doin' is carried out absolutely right, like perfectly. And when they finally come to thinkin' that just maybe, just maybe, they've really got it down pat, they wind up not even trustin' their own eyes. The poor slobs continue to look, and look, and look, not in the least bit certain of what they're actually starin' at. They're stuck in a rut doubtin' everything they see, or even hear for that matter. So how do you like them apples?"

Adam knew he was wasting his time before he even sought a reaction from this fellow. His bench sharing observer of the Dupont scene was too casual a type either to buy into his astuteness or turn sympathetic once he'd bared his own very pressing personal problems. He was right.

"Man. How'd you ever come by such a weird view of things? You are sure one fucked up mother. For me, life is all about hangin' out an' not bein' stuck in some kinda' dumb groove. Hangin' out in all kinds'a cool, laid back ways. And you do it however you like, because you are free. Free, man. Free. Christ! Ain't you ever heard'a free will?"

Adam had an urge to pop the creepy guy right in his upstart face. Make him share in the pain. How could it be that such a simple minded clown had privileged immunity from his kind of ailment? But Adam wasn't annoyed enough to go that far. Anyway, he considered that perhaps his Horla selected the very best human types for bedevilment.

"Yeah. I've heard of it."

"So?"

"So it's bullshit. Want to know why you're so damned free-willed you got to be an unkempt, big-mouthed freak? It comes down to it bein' a copycat thing. Some nitwit out there who was never put together well enough in the first place to amount to very much had no option but to drop out and settle for his unendowed self. However much he tried, he just couldn't cut it. Then all the other similarly handicapped jerks, guys like you with no better prospects than his, put into play their only natural talent, that of imitation, and fell into lockstep with their new role model, a similarly minded jackass. That, Mac, is all there is to it. The simple truth is that no way, no way ever, could someone like you free will yourself into measurin' up and amounting to something worthwhile."

"You fucking well through?"

"I never wanted to get started in the first place. All of this was your idea. Remember?"

Smarting from his put-down, the seedy one rose from the bench and begun to amble away. Adam watched as he melded with people moving along the Connecticut Avenue corridor. Odd though, that in the course of making off, as far as Adam could track him, he'd managed to touch one or other sandal to just about every transverse crack in the sidewalk. As often as he'd tried, Adam could never do something like that. Not even when he was nine years old or so and the Horla had forced this aversion upon him. Or rather was this idiosyncrasy just another avoidance compulsion that Rogoff had been inclined to diagnose? Whatever it amounted to, omen or symptom, it annoyed him to watch the receding scruffy figure execute the precise maneuvers he was incapable of performing himself. Adam watched him tread upon crack after taboo'd crack, as if to spite him, until mercifully the fellow passed from sight.

It was then he remembered that there were all of those other patterns of childhood behavior that required him to be inordinately certain that even the most innocent and trivial actions were reliably carried out.

Topping the list were spellings and punctuation marks. Especially the circumflex and cedilla punctuations for his French lessons which, unaccountably, he was required to painstakingly impress over and over again into his home-work book until the writing surfaces were holed clear through.

Christ, he thought, only a month before he'd been up in the attic looking for office records and come across those same fifty-year-old lesson books from public school. He had run his fingers across the ancient scrawlings, felt the harsh imprints, and seen the wretched perforations. He turned the pages to examine their reverse surfaces. It was evident that time and again they had been attacked with enough ink for it to bleed right through to the fol-lowing page. Held up to a mirror, the back surfaces were imprinted deeply enough to be easily read from behind. And once raised to eye level, some of the perforations were so large they permitted a good view of whatever else one might want to search for in his attic.

The problem went beyond French lessons. Anything he had to write by hand was affected by that same perfection aimed enslavement. And of all of this, no one, not at home or in school, was in the least bit aware.

All of these years later, on a park bench in Dupont Circle, Adam remembered that old fool math teacher, a certain Mister Burns. He could envision that red faced ignoramus seizing one of Adam's tortured pennings and waving it in the air so that the other students might admire the horrid evidence of Adam's privately held agony. Burns wanted them to understand that this kind of attention to detail was required if they were to make it in the real world. Adam, had believed that he was possessed by the devil himself, and yet here was this misguided teacher rhapsodizing over the awful work product of his bewitchment.

Appearances in Dupont Circle had changed. Scents of spring and precocious outcroppings might still be there but the air was no longer optimistically inspired. Adam continued to sit on the bench and remained annoyed by the long passed Burns, but now he was also getting piqued by certain remembrances of his mother. Had she not been too kindly in her forbearance, too supportive, when these crippling habits of his had first surfaced? Could she not guess what was actually happening to him? Did not this austere, but tender woman, at least suspect that by yielding to his insistence to personally verify the accuracy of everything he set to paper, she was cultivating this problematic tendency and making it worse? Overwhelmed by maternal desire to be responsive to his needs, even though page after page set before her showed unmistakable signs of near on fragmentation under the ferocious onslaught of his repetitive pennings. This solicitously indulgent woman had merely squeezed her pince-nez ever so carefully to the bridge of her nose, and sat there ready to affirm, on the night before each new school day, that every one of those abominable words and punctuation marks had been correctly inscribed. Only then would Adam's anxiety be allayed sufficiently for the lessons to be secured in his briefcase and carried to the next day's classes.

What could she have been making of his atrocious behavior? Was it no more than a zealous son's exaggerated effort to get passing grades or even, to excel? Could she not realize that something sick or evil had taken hold here? Or did she just consider her son beset by one of those oft-alleged childhood habits kids can be expected to "grow" out of? In any event, some kind of professional help was out of the question. They were too poor for anything like that, even if the need for psychiatric evaluation had been suspected.

But grow out of it he did. Adam couldn't recall exactly when this had happened but certainly not before he'd stumbled across the Horla business. There it was, by chance, on a seldom visited back shelf of the local library, a dusty old copy of the spooky de Maupassant tale. To be possessed, much as the fellow in the book, by a shadowy kind of evil took easy hold of his beleaguered young mind.

Then, strangely enough, acceding to the Horla's dominion over him, Adam's compulsive habits actually started to ease off during his senior high school years. By the time he'd graduated college and been conscripted into the army, they were gone. It was not until very much later, after getting married, that there might occur a special occasion when he'd yank the front door shut more than just a single time, and a bit too vigorously, especially at night, or before heading out of town, like to an airport. There were also other unaccountable times when such maneuvers were executed rigorously enough for the hinges of the door to be at risk of coming away. But that was the extent of it until out of nowhere, his old affliction--demoralizingly revitalized, persistent, and with apparently enhanced powers--took him over again.

But now there was no kindly, indulgent mother to be counted upon. No one to affirm that whatever he did was being done just right. There existed no maternal dispensation empowering him to break away, after a reasonable time, from his accursed rituals of almost unending repetitive checking. There was no way for him to measure what he was doing over and over in the seclusion of his home, or embarrassingly enough, even when out in public.

The sun was on the the verge of slipping below the tree line. A warm day had turned chill, and here sat Adam, a grown man, close to tears, still fixed on remembering his ruddy-faced math teacher, and a loving but helpless mother.

He knew that any presumption that these were just discomforting reminiscences of awkward rites of youthful passage were off the mark. To the contrary. He understood those childhood years full well. They'd amounted to nothing less than a gargantuan struggle to succeed at school in spite of his profoundly handicapping psychological impediment.

But even before the compulsions had taken hold, his life had never been a very satisfying experience. It seemed that from the very outset of self awareness there'd abided an odd sense of unease. So then, he wondered, by drawing upon those earlier times, might he finally unearth the true genesis of his disorder?

Adam's bench-place mullings headed further back. Back to oft recurrent, unpleasant, recollections of an infantile imprisonment behind a crib railing. Could he have been more than three at the time? Probably not. And yet his rudimentary mind had already brimmed with resentment. After all, was he significantly different from them--his mother and father? And yet, they'd caged him. He'd wanted out of there, to be free of his confinement. How outrageous not to be treated as an equal, but rather to be locked away. Was it a wonder that this haplessly evolving, but penned creature, should wind up unduly dependent upon them?

When the day finally arrived for him to be released from this protective arrangement and sent to school, the mere announcement of it was sufficient to consume him with terrible trepidation over the impending cleavage. What else could be expected but that when finally carted off to school by his mother he'd bolt for home as soon as his kindergarten teacher had turned her back? His mother found him sobbing at the door to their apartment.

An imperfect representation of the past? Why then, could he still see so vividly those other five year olds in the classroom he'd rushed away from? There they were, busy at their ridiculous assigned tasks, layering coat after coat of smelly paint upon glass jars and empty milk bottles. He could smell the paint, and recapture the odor of the globs of white mucilage those elfin creatures had smeared across the backs of silly cardboard cutouts.

Regarding himself as different, awash in anxiety and distraught by consignment to the company of such clumsy little fumbling dwarfs, what recourse did he have but to race for home and the protective company of solicitous grown ups, his true counterparts?

That same fidgety mind was engaged now, right there in Dupont Circle. Adam was confronted with the probability that his current dilemma was not a question of some sort of temporary psychological setback. This stood to be much more serious because the Horla's reappearance was clear evidence that his brain, secondary to what had been caused to fester within it, had endured in a uniqely fragile state. Boastful myths of self control and self determination could not apply here because his brain, unlike most other tissues of his body, was no longer running its own program. Adam was not unaware of those inborn biologically predetermined genetic flaws that could ease people into various kinds of premature decrepitude. This was differnt. Something told him his troubles were from outside, not from anywhere inside him. He had a longstanding basis for this conviction that the Horla was invading him in order, eventually, to take him over entirely.

Three

The office could wait. His personal problems came first. Right now it was best to walk a bit, even get a little shopping done while he took stock of his all-consuming dilemma.

His first step after leaving the bench was to head back towards Rogoff, but that was a mistake. There were very few shops in that direction and why be tempted to get embroiled in some kind of a heated putdown? Telling the old man off for his bum steer on what to anticipate from Prozac would be counterproductive. However much he wanted to unload on his doctor he still needed him for guidance. Anyway, how much straight talk could you really expect from a physician these days? Just like Rogoff had confided to him, there were simply no rules on how physicians might advise their patients. Best to let the matter ride and if things did turn out badly, he could always take the bastard to court and sue him.

So downtown towards the commercial and shopping areas was the better way to head. But he would be careful not to tread on any of those mischievous cracks in the sidewalk along the way.

Reactivated was a need for reassurance regarding the whereabouts of his wallet.. Following the disappearance of the scruffy one, he'd fingered for it in his right rear pants pocket. After all, these days, one couldn't be too careful. But now a second order of checking was required and of a different kind, its purpose to determine not only whether the earlier verification of the wallet's presence had been correct, but also whether that type of confirmation was valid in present circumstance. After all, there did exist the presumably credible possibility of the wallet's dislodgement in the course of his coming off the bench. In all truth, however, he knew there could be no reasonable explanation for his imminently deplorable antics other than an abiding need to obey the Horla.

Reaching around, Adam drew the wallet from his back pocket, raised it before him and stared. There existed no alternative. The Horla's directives were compelling and non-challengeable. But having this well-worn brown leather object right before his eyes in no way convinced him. To merely see it, or even feel it, was not the same as being persuaded of anything. Although this sort of thing had been going on for months now, there always seemed some further undertaking needed as justification to move on to other matters.

Ever innovative and inventive, he was not to be stymied in this regard. And so in short order he'd decided that were he to explore the innards of his wallet and have the benefit sometime later of recalling its specific contents, there'd be some better, if still not overwhelming grounds, for a measure of reassurance that he'd come as close as was feasible to a bona fide conviction of having retained the god-damned thing.

Reassurance? For him? Hardly. Adam no longer had confidence about anything.

He opened the wallet and looked inside of it, carefully examining the contents. Charge cards: Exxon, American Express, Visa...as well as some cash. They were all there. But now there was something else, an obligation quite apart from mere substantiation of the wallet itself. Everything, ordinarily relegated to that wallet needed also to be confirmed as being there. So painstakingly, he ferreted through it: certain business cards, penned memoranda, hastily scrawled telephone numbers long buried and not dialed for years, including those of persons abroad and local. Some belonged to faces remembered. Of others, Adam no longer had any memory at all. Finally, satisfied for the moment that all these things were in order, he could then return the wallet to that same right rear pants pocket and secure it by fastening the appropriate button.

Next, tentatively, he moved further away from the bench, but not before completing one quick rearwards grope and a feel for the wallet's bulging presence. This would not put an end to it. He was always in the habit of palpating this particular right rear trouser pocket any time he crossed a street, and on innumerable other anticipated, as well as unpredictable, occasions. Rogoff had said that what eluded him was something called "a proper sense of closure". Some help, that little nugget of psychobabble.

To be adrift with no particular destination in mind was comforting. Adam wished for a moment that there existed no house to return to. A house with all of those wretched doors needing to be made fast, and the electric appliances and gas fixtures having to be overseen or accounted for. Perhaps to own nothing and be spared the responsibility for safeguarding anything at all might release him from such strangleholds. It was a novel thought but he may have managed precisely that, and gotten along pretty damned well, when as a young army recruit he'd only been responsible for what was issued him. Or were those his better days simply because the Horla had not been patriotic enough to get himself mustered alongside him?

So divestment was his out? The way to beat this rap? Could he be like all those fired-up anti-materialistic ne'er-do-wells hanging out right there in Dupont Circle? Just get down and dirty, and as threadbare as they were? Well, he could forget all of that right now. What could he be thinking? Try and lay that one on any of his uptight, appearance oriented, Republican clients. There'd be hell to pay. And yet, it was a neat idea. Enough to have him rueful over the irony of such a ploy. Here, on the one hand was this, maybe the only way to cheat the devil, a duplicitous devil set on taking him over ever more completely. But then, there were his hard-nosed Republican meal-tickets to be reckoned with, unscrupulous guys themselves who needed him big-time and were sure to be turned off by such an over-arching remedy.

Well how about that! It was getting to be quite a day. For he had another provocative thought. What he remembered was reading somewhere that certain people with cancer had kept their devilish malignancies at bay by seizing upon every conceivable opportunity to laugh their forlorn heads off. And right up to their demise. They'd even lay around watching old Marx Brothers movies. So why not pull off a stunt like that himself? Organize some kind of a terminal laughfest, going not so far as to laugh himself to death but at least into some sort of even keeled existence beyond the reach of his tormentor. Far fetched, perhaps, but worth thinking about while he proceeded downtown.

Along the way, he had further reminiscences of better times. He now recalled that even before those army years, especially during college, he'd experience no compulsive behavior at all for months at a stretch. And to think of it, those were probably times that found him preoccupied with sex. So sex, then? Might a patron saint for chasing tail be his benevolent talisman? It might just be. For certain it was true that when too much of it did finally land him up on Rogoff's couch that first time, any compulsive behavior, especially of the kind he suffered from now, was not part of the picture. And no question about it, he was much more miserable now than back then and would gladly swap situations. After all, sex had its obvious rewards. But these days all he had was torment from pulling doors ever more tightly, staring at stove burners, and feeling his rear end for the presence of that stupid wallet. Besides which, if he could beat this thing, even a little, by romancing someone, that was a damned site more attractive than some statistically half-assed sixty percent improvement on Rogoff's little green and yellow pills.

The appeal of such a remedy was enough to importune immediate action. Searching the passing scene on Connecticut Avenue, he thought to test this zesty little concept by focusing on chance passers-by for any signs of suitable female allurement. Almost at once he was rewarded by the appearance of two rapidly moving examples. One, bobbing along on outrageously elevated stiletto heels, had no recourse for sake of balance but to swing her hips and unsupported breasts in ways that would provoke any viable male. The other, quite petite, was eating on the run and making a hasty but determined effort to alternately lick or mouth away the frosty summit of a chocolate delight of some kind. But he was dead in the water. All he felt was an irresistible inclination to run still another check on his right rear pants pocket. The possibility of diversionary sexual incitement remained strictly theoretical.

Then he realized that during the last few months, following a protracted period of marital discord and divorce proceedings, he'd had no such yearnings at all. He was inclined to attribute such a falling off to the marital conflict, as well as to a few unusually tedious and newly undertaken political commitments. The possibility of a more ominous problem with his libido had been discounted. But now he was confronted with hardly disputable evidence of an even more insidious reach of the Horla. That the bouncing extravagance of female buxomness and other incitingly suggestive acts were no longer capable of evoking any sort of arousal was indeed scary and a bitter pill to swallow. Chalk up one more for the Horla?

As for the other pills, the little green and yellow ones Rogoff was pushing? All things considered, could they conceivably provide him with an out? And what about his newly dreamed-up crackpot remedies, those of self-divestment, mirth, or womanizing? Would they also fall short, in all truth being too fanciful? Or too impotent? As impotent, maybe, as he was now himself?

A guy, he thought, could just take so much. What the hell. He'd chance it and swallow down some more of Rogoff's stuff. Although he wasn't supposed to take Prozac again until later in the day, and was wary of bringing on another of what may already have been some kind of unusual reaction, he reached into his pocket for a capsule. Briefly hesitating, he thrust it into his mouth and swallowed resolutely. It felt like a desperate hardening of some sort of resolve. A devil may care resolve?

He'd walked far enough to have come upon the Mayflower Hotel with its gleaming, fast revolving front doors. Entry seemed reasonable enough, perhaps even called for. Whirling his way into the lobby, he spotted almost immediately a cluster of comfortable looking armchairs over to the left, well away from the crowded reception area. He'd seat himself and remain ensconced, awaiting further developments. At the back of his mind was the troubling possibility of another drug reaction. A relatively safe spot in a public place, like the one he was heading for now, should work quite well. Nevertheless, he didn't want to take any chances with this second cast upon uncertain pharmacological waters. For to chance anything at all would be strange and unusual behavior for this ordinarily purposeful and rigidly organized man.

He sat there for perhaps an hour mostly watching varied and odd sorts at the check-in counter. In each instance, based upon appearances, he'd estimate who might be convention-bound or just in town for sight-seeing. After awhile he sized up one particular guy. He was nattily dressed in a dark double-breasted, pin-striped suit and held pretty much to one corner of the lobby. It looked like he was searching the faces of just about everyone passing by. Could he be meeting up with a dame? Probably not. He was staring at everyone, men and women alike. They all drew his scrutiny. So before dozing off Adam had settled on his being some sort of misdirected diplomatic type, or maybe even the house detective.

"You checking in sir?"

A heavy-handed prodding was a rude kind of arousal, not befitting a place aspiring to be newly up-market. All the same, Adam realized he'd been correct in his last assessment of the dark suited one, who was now hanging over him and burrowing into his left shoulder quite determinedly.

"What's it to yuh?"

"These chairs, sir, are not for just anybody who comes along to sleep in. They're for our own patrons, their guests, and those who may have appointments at the hotel."

"Do I look like I'm homeless? And have you any idea whom you're dealin' with? You're looking at the chairman of the New York fundraising committee of the Republican party."

Adam, erupting belligerently from his slouched position was high atop his horse, intending neither to come down voluntarily, nor to be unseated by his persistent inquisitor.

"Then you're meeting someone, are you?"

"Nope."

"Sir. Please. Just a little cooperation, if you will. Perhaps you have some sort of an I.D.?"

"Whether I do or I don't is none of your business."

"I'd really appreciate your showing it to me."

Like a bulldog, the guy was unrelenting in his obstinacy.

"Look buddy, I don't need an I.D. I know exactly who I am. What's more, this is a public place. Right? So unless you have some kind of privileged exemption or know of regulations to the contrary, just buzz off. Maybe you can find somebody else's business to mind. It's damned sure not gonna be mine. Savvy?"

Adam had an established flair for being obnoxious and bringing out the worst in people.

"I'll be back shortly and with the manager."

"I can't wait."

Since Adam had had nothing particular in mind coming into this place, the pressing question was whether an impending row with hotel management over the security officer's overstepping his bounds was the best way to be running down present time. He decided probably not. So on his feet once more, he fast-stepped his way over to the concierge's desk and delivered what he intended to be a huffy last word on his possibly impending eviction from the lobby.

"Tell your manager, if he's interested, that I'll be in the bar, where I was headed in the first place. And remind the guy in stripes that my last words were `I can't wait'".

"And you are?"

"Me, myself and I."

It was vintage Adam, and lest anyone read him too well, cryptic enough for those unfamiliar with his ways to be utterly confused.

But why he should be headed for the bar was another of the day's unfolding mysteries. Especially since the kind of watering hole he now proceeded to enter looked to be no more than a structural afterthought, an awkward add-on, barely accommodating a half dozen people and almost crowding out the entranceway to an equally small but bustling restaurant catering to those needing some kind of a sit-down place where business luncheons could be hastily consumed. Also, there was the fact that according to the printed warnings for Prozac, still lodged in his pocket, he wasn't supposed to have any alcohol around the time he'd be taking his brain-busting drug. But as far as he could tell, what Prozac he'd swallowed only a short while ago wasn't doing anything for him and he sorely needed a lift. So what the hell, he'd go for it and have himself a stiff drink.

Minutes later he was perched on a bar stool and alternately staring down into his single malt or at his image reflecting from a mirror behind the bar. No doubt about it. The life of that sad faced guy was a shambles ever since the divorce.

But why, he asked himself, should he be feeling guilty about that? After all, wasn't his wife the one who wouldn't tango? Right. The damned woman hunkered down and wouldn't go along with his heading out of town so often, or being hustled by all of those oily, groping congressmen and horny aides he had to work with.

But what'd she expect? Christ. She kept busy enough preserving her good looks and never shied away from showing how well stacked she was. What'd she think was gonna happen? She sure did nothing to play down those big boobs of hers. Guilt? Not on that score. Not by a long shot. Okay, maybe for foolin' around once in awhile himself. But what the hell. That was ancient history long before they parted ways. He'd put a stop to it right after his first go 'round with Rogoff. And all that stuff was light years ago. So when he stopped to think about it, there really wasn't much for him to feel guilty about. Not about any of that, anyway.

No. For big time guilt feelings he'd have to consider the time Rogoff first unearthed them. Back to the age of ten or eleven and he'd jerked off once or twice and started, just for once, to enjoy himself a little. But all it took was for Arney, that creepy spoilsport friend of his, to ruin it all by declaring that if he kept it up, the word around school was eventually you'd go blind. Not that that ever stopped him. Hell, back then, what kind of fun was there, otherwise? And it was all so quick and easy, and kinda pure. But Arney sure did put a crimp in it. Made him feel so absolutely lousy about what he might be doing to himself.

So, for the first time in his life, there was all that guilt. And for what? For unadulterated bullshit. No wonder he was fair game for the Horla when that one first showed up. Hey. How about that? Was the Horla just some kind of punishment? Self-punishment for the dedicated little masturbator he'd become? It could add up. Might even be Freudian enough to satisfy old Rogoff.

Or was that miserable little kid with the embarrassing acne, just imagining God had spotted him at his clandestine self-pleasuring? Found him in flagrant violation of some kind of big-time taboo and decided to nail him for it once and for all? Incredible? Not really. Maybe things were starting to come together a little.

It didn't appear, though, as far as he could surmise from his reflected image, that he'd been fired up very much by that little brainstorm. There were no telltale signs of such a breakthrough. All he saw was his same old preoccupied and sullen puss. But now, projecting back at him, just to the right of his own image, was another reflection.

A young woman had taken form and was beginning to draw on her cigarette. One whiff and she needed telling off.

"Hey. You mind not doing that?"

"What?"

"Blowing smoke at me. I don't like it."

"Sorry, old top, but in this bar it's not illegal. In fact, it's still legal in any bar."

Adam's reaction to that disclaimer was quick and inspired.

"I tell you what. Back off with the cigarette and I'll pay for the drink."

"Agreed."

As she outed her cigarette Adam declared his obligation.

"Hey, mister bartender. I'm coverin' the lady's tab."

Turning back to the mirror but prompted now to make a more studied examination of the woman's reflection, he could appreciate that she easily had more going for her than those other two, the ones he'd ogled earlier along Connecticut Avenue. He could also see that she had a small blue badge pinned to her blouse. But even were it feasible to overcome the difficulty in making something out at a distance doubled by reflection, never could he solve the problem of having to read the badge's inscription backwards to decipher her name and organization. So he twisted around and bent over to peer at it.

"Hi there, Miranda. How yuh doin'?"

"Not too badly. And you?"

He decided to be up front and reveal himself. Why not see what could come of making it that kind of a day?

"Crummy. Real crummy. My life's in a helluva mess. But let me guess. You're either waitin' for somebody, or sittin' here in a bum mood too. Right?"

"I'm not waiting for anyone. At least, not any longer. My girlfriend just called to say she couldn't make it."

"Well then, admit it. You're also feelin' bum."

"How does that figure?"

"Well who'd be happy like this... sittin' on a bar... and all by their lonesome?"

Miranda reached over. He thought she did it rather softly, and patted the back of his hand.

"Who's alone? I've got you now. Have I not?"

Adam, for once, seemed flustered. "Really?"

"Are you planning to hurry your drink and split?"

He quickly recovered. "Hardly."

"Precisely. I thought not. And might you be finished eyeing me in that mirror you've been just about glued to?"

"I can't. You've got me bowled over."

"All right then, unless you are from outer space or some kind of weirdo, you're mine."

"I'm weird. Trust me. Very, very, weird."

"Sorry to hear that. You had me fooled. I simply took you for a nice old garden variety ogler."

Adam couldn't waste another second fencing with such a dame. No gal had ever come on to him this boldly, much less such a hazel-eyed, good looker. Although her implicitly open-ended overture was enticing, he would hardly have expected it from a gal so primly decked out. And yet there was a provocative air at play here. Miranda's nose, quite narrow and well configured had a kind of upstart swerve to it. And when she spoke, her lips, although thin and delicate, managed to produce adventurously cheery sounds bearing the crisp trace of a kind of upstart British accent. Hair? Ash blond and shoulder length. Age? A little hard to estimate but along far enough for the bloom to have backed off a bit, but that only added to the attraction of certain all-knowing looks she seemed to have turned in his direction. Inevitable that he should find himself picturing her figure, drawn no doubt by her concealment of most of it. And hard not to imagine how he might be affected if she had chosen rather to flaunt it. As it was, the way her blouse filled out was telling enough.

Adam resumed, a bit awkwardly. "You in the dress business, or something?"

"Why? Do I look like a model?"

"I just thought..."

"I'm in event management. Do publicity, you know, run ads and things. Mostly for small but some big organizations. I just finished a conference here at the hotel."

"And you've got yourself an accent."

"That's an odd way to put it. We're from England, originally. My parents and I, that is. It's where I grew up and actually where I studied graphic arts. But when we came over here I switched to what I do now. It pays a lot more and allows me to still be decorous about whatever I'm into."

"Yeah?"

She countered with a pretty good imitation.

"Yeah."

Adam found the need to apologize. "I'm a little rusty."

"Taking too much iron, are you?"

"You're a piece'a work. You know that? Don't act like you don't know what's goin' on here and make it even harder for me. It's been a long time and I've never been much good at finessin' a pick-up."

"Poor little man. Look here. Would you like to nibble at something? We could appropriate that table over there before someone else gets it. Would that be acceptable? Yes? Lovely. And allow me to carry your drink."

"What is it with you? I'm supposed to be the weird

one. No? So lay off. You're not gonna' carry anything. If you don't mind, I'll handle the glasses."

"Such a gentleman."

Having waved off her bold offering, Adam arranged for the table and saw to it that their drinks were moved over. Miranda, soon ensconced at a table happening to be set for four, appeared delighted.

"Isn't this quite marvelous and so much better than that smoky old bar? But confess. You're expecting someone else, aren't you. I've noted that this particular table has four place settings."

"Look, kiddo. I just drifted in here by accident. I'm not meeting up with anyone. And if you don't mind, take off the silly badge. It makes it look like you're out to sell me something. Just assume, whatever it is, I'm buyin' and we don't need to advertise it any."

"But that's what I do...advertise. You've forgotten, already?"

"Gotcha. Okay, listen up. I'm off duty. You're off duty. How about us startin' all over and takin' it from there?"

Miranda decided to go along. She detached her nameplate and slipped it into her shoulderbag, all the while staring at him expectantly as if needing to set some kind of a course.

"So then... what next?"

"Well you're right about it bein' more comfortable over here but I'm not all that hungry so why don't you order whatever you want? I'll stay with my drink, and maybe munch on something later on."

"Not on your life. I'm requesting combo's for the two of us."

"Okay, sweetheart. Take charge. Because from here on

in I'm for relaxin' and not bein' my usual kind of control freak. Although I might have to get myself reborn to pull that one off."

Miranda had been so busy giving the waiter her order that she seemed not to have been listening. But that completed, she turned and fixed on him.

"Well then, capital! It's on the way and you are just dying to dump on me. Aren't you, though? So go ahead. Ventilate. You'll find me a splendid listener. And if you simply must get born again, we can imagine this to be our very own little nursery."

"Unless you pay through the nose for it, ventilating isn't supposed to work. At least that's what my analyst told me."

"So slip me a five note, mein herr, und ve can begin. As they say, lay it all on me."

"I wouldn't expect an English girl to be putting it quite that way."

"Welcome to the age of global enlightenment. But why are you changing the subject? We were about to get ourselves reborn. Were we not?"

Adam paused to think it over.

"What I'm tryin' to say is that I'd like to feel the way it was about everything, even ordinary things, when I was fresh out the box. Do you know what I mean? Nothing turns me on anymore. I'm as old as the world itself."

"Are you that depressed or simply jaded?"

"Who would know the difference? The best way to put it, there's a monkey on my back and he's got me down. It's no fun. You see, I don't jerk his chain. He jerks mine. And makes me do things I don't want to do."

"That's ridiculous."

"Really? How'd you like to meet him?"

Adam summoned up an image of his Horla. It hovered around Miranda's head and leered malevolently from a curl of smoke.

"What does your analyst say about all this silliness?"

"Silliness? This deal's as heavy as it gets. What he says is that I'm just your garden variety obsessive-compulsive checker and starts me off on Prozac. I took my first two pills today. The odd thing is that right after the first dose I got to feelin' real neat for maybe fifteen minutes or so. Then, with the second pill, nothin', nothin' at all. Another thing..."

"I can hardly wait."

"Just so you know. It could be I'm into a boy kinda let down. Like for instance, you've probably got more and then some of everything that counts, but this here guy is not set to trot."

"How unfortunate. But however equipped, you do come with a name, do you not?"

"Sorry about that. You've been messin' around with Adam Carter."

"Well Adam old boy, I think you're getting a good bit ahead of yourself. And as long as we're into truth telling, when I spotted you in the bar, and you looked so low in spirits, I wondered if you would consider some pleasant diversion. You see, the girl I was supposed to meet, my old friend Delphine Hadley? We were scheduled for the Kennedy Center this evening, and now, not only do I find myself with an extra ticket but I abhor, absolutely abhor going alone to such things. Do you follow me?"

"I'll be damned. I get to pick you up because you need an escort. Cool. Real cool. But no good for what's left of my ego. You know that?"

"Please don't take it like that. Not for a second did I consider you as gruffy as you were letting on. And if I didn't think you were the right sort of person, we wouldn't be sitting here together. So how about it? Are you engaged for the evening? Or would you possibly fancy a concert?"

"No I'm not `engaged'. Anyway, not until now. And I do like classical music. But if I go along with the deal, you'll be pickin' up the tab for the sandwiches. I'm in it only for the drinks. Take it or leave it."

"You are hard-nosed, aren't you? But what can a poor girl do in a desperate situation. Anyway. What do you do? Stockbroker? Lawyer? Accountant? Indian chief?"

"I raise money for politicians and lobbyists."

Miranda got a rise out of that.

"Dear Lord. I've misled myself. And fallen in with a man of no scruples."

"Come on now. Expect me to believe you buy your own copy? Don't tell me you stand behind the ads you run."

"Very well. Touche." She raised her glass. "To birds of comparable feather."

"Nightingales or vultures?"

"The kind that shouldn't need to sing for their supper. So do you mind if I start on my nourishment? I'm practically starving. And in case you didn't notice, Sir Grumpy. What your kind calls `the eats', have arrived."

"Sure kiddo. Go right ahead. But this bird doesn't sing anymore. And he sure doesn't chirp any either. Like you want to hear something really pathetic? The last coupla' nights I haven't even gone up to bed. Because I knew damned well I was gonna hate, absolutely hate gettin' up in the morning to deal with another one of my kinda' days. And all because I'm into what my mind guy calls this checking business. I've got to verify everything, and not just once, but lotsa times. And at night when I'm close to turning in I do it more than ever. So who wants days or nights like that? Hey. You hearin' any a' this?"

Miranda had consumed half her sandwich and now seemed to focus her entire attention on a side order of potato salad. She barely glanced at him.

"Sure, sure. Of course. Poor dear. Poor, poor, dear."

And resumed her meal taking.

"You're not impressed with my particular misery?"

"But I am. I am."

She proceeded to tackle the other half of her sandwich.

"Press on. Press on. I'm really all ears. Do continue. But I can't help thinking that what you're learning is how it feels to be, now don't take this the wrong way, but maybe... like Jewish. As I understand it you can get used to it. And take suffering for granted. Even look forward, eventually, to the bad days. Say. Mind if I borrow half your sandwich? I'm still a little hungry."

"Go ahead. I've no appetite at all. But your off the mark with your presumption. As far as I know, I'm not the least bit Jewish."

She'd wolfed his half down, hardly coming up for air.

"You could have fooled me. Sorry about that. And Adam, please be assured that I sympathize entirely with what you've been going through. But try and look at it another way. At present you are not at home. There's nothing here needing to be checked out except yours very truly. And we are pointed towards a delightful evening. After we depart these premises we can stroll over to the Kennedy Center, take the elevator up top to the terrace lounge, and perhaps have another little refreshment. Then, why not a nice little meander around the outdoor deck until performance time? Maybe even an arm-in-arm one? What do you say? Think you can handle it? And may the devil take your nasty little old monkey."

He decided to confide his worst thoughts.

"Actually. He just might be the devil himself."

"Then it's high time we praised the dear Lord and hoped for some kind of a sign."

Without asking for permission, the young woman who seemed to have an answer for everything, snatched the other half of his sandwich. Adam nibbled a few peanuts, sipped his scotch, and watched her eat. They were, he thought, a peculiar pair. But still, it was legitimate, in the sense of being quite in line with how odd this new week had been shaping up.

New week? Why did he consider it to be a new week? Well because he'd thought it Monday, not suspecting until this moment, that it was something else. Some other day. But which? He found it hard to tell. Well then, how to find out? He'd noted that Miranda had been toting a copy of the New York Times.

"I see you've got the paper. Mind if I take a peek?"

"Your interest in me is exhausted already?"

"Not on your life. I just need a stock quote."

Christ. Before he'd flipped to the business section he'd already seen a heading and it wasn't Monday at all, but Friday. How could he have made such a stupid mistake? Then it came to him. Great. Just great. His first dose of the stuff had turned him on to Dupont Circle in an irrational way and now the second one had made him lose all sense of time. Or could the lapse be due to an ill-advised combination of Prozac and alcohol? After all, he'd been

given fair warning not to combine them. Anyway, he decided that from then on, no more booze. At the same time
a bigger concern might be that the Horla, set now upon
bolder strokes, had begun to grab for ever bigger chunks
of his brain. What possibilities! To be taken over by either
drug or demon. And each capable of scuttling his mind.

Miranda was curious.

"How's it going? Make any money?"

"Great. We're up three points."

"You don't seem very thrilled about it."

"Like I just finished telling you. Nothing turns me on."

"That's so sad... Hey. There's just one bite left. Want it?"

"No. Go ahead. Then we can take off."

"No desert?"

"Let's wait until we're at the Kennedy Center."

"Good thinking."

In line with their understanding, each handed a credit
card to the waiter who was back in a few minutes with
separate charge slips, Adam's for the drinks, hers for the
two sandwiches. Miranda penned her figures and committed her signature by a hasty scrawl. Peeling off the
customer's copy she slipped it into her purse. Then she
waited for Adam to follow suit so that both their charge
slips could be turned over to the waiter who was standing
nearby at the ready. But nothing that casual or ordinary
was proceeding across the table. The tip of his ballpoint
was being directed back and forth, so as to doggedly trace
and retrace the itemized figures posted to his bill. It didn't
take long for her to express puzzlement over these antics.

"Something wrong? Were you overcharged?"

"No. It adds up fine. I'm just making sure."

"How sure must you be? You seem to have added up

those figures three or four times already. And you've only the charges for two drinks. So what does it amount to?"

"Twelve seventy-five, including tax and a three buck tip."

"So sign it and we're on our way. I'm looking forward to our little walk."

"Not just yet. I can't."

"You ill or something?"

"No. I just need to look at it, go over it... a little more."

"I'm not comprehending you. Are you seriously telling me that those simple little numbers don't add up entirely to your satisfaction?"

"It's not the numbers. And to tell the truth, which in case you haven't noticed, is what I've been trying to get across to you, nothing's ever entirely to my satisfaction. How could it be when I'm not dead sure of anything? I guess you haven't really been listening."

"Fiddlesticks. Now let us not be unreasonable."

Reaching over, she grabbed for Adam's charge slip and after no more than a glance at it, flipped it back to him.

"Look. Take my word for it. It's perfect. Sign the blessed thing and we will extract ourselves from here."

"Good deal. There now... it's all done. Thank's a bunch. I'm real grateful to yuh. Otherwise, we could've been at it quite awhile."

"You're obliged to me?"

"Why not? I owe you. Don't I? And you wanna know something else? I'm thinkin' you could come in real handy."

Almost proudly, he surrendered their completed tabs to the waiter. But they were not to leave that fast because Miranda was to be confronted by an odd series of movements starting up directly across from her.

"Mind telling me what you're about now?"

"Well, what we have here is my wallet. And what I'm doing is observing it and getting ready to put my credit card back inside, along with the charge slip. But I need to be sure that nothing falls out before I've got it back in my right rear pants pocket."

"There's nothing amiss on top the table. Right?"

"Right."

"Or the floor. Right?"

"If you say so."

"What do you mean, `if you say so'? Don't you accept my word for it?"

"Well, sort of. But thanks again, anyway."

Miranda looked on disbelievingly as ever so carefully, Adam got up and buried the wallet in his right rear pocket. Then he tapped his rear end a few times in line with his usual custom.

She smiled and touched his hand once more, and differently from that first time. It was in a comforting sort of way.

"Come on Adam. Let us wander."

Four

Miranda had him by the arm, drawing him southward, as soon as they were out on Connecticut Avenue. It made him uncomfortable to realize that her somewhat sympathetic gesture had reminded him of another experienced long ago. There was something redolently familiar in the way he inclined now to let her take charge. That same kind of old comfort had surfaced when she'd verified his bar tab. It didn't take him long to grasp its underpinnings. Had he not forced that same kind of pathetic favoring from an indulgent mother when the Horla made first appearance? But best to ease off on such thoughts or their evening might have an undesireable downturn.

He sounded her out on the matter at hand.

"So what's with the concert?"

"Mahler, the ninth symphony. Lorin Maazel will be conducting."

"I saw Bernstein do it years ago with the New York Philharmonic. Never heard Maazel live. Only recordings. He's supposed to be some kind of enfant terrible. See kiddo?

Never would'a thought it, would you? Got yourself a real musical aficionado, haven't you though?"

"Well I go to concerts once in a while but I'm just a peasant with regard to symphonies, or opera either. I'm ashamed to say my musical taste is more apt to run to Bob Dylan. It's just that someone I know gave me two tickets. Then I asked my friend, and now you. There's surely no point in their going to waste. But you know, I've always had the feeling that situations turn out just as they're supposed to."

"My lucky day?"

"Don't get carried away, Adam."

"Okay... Just let me know when it's time to make my first pass."

"Remember? I'm an English girl. We behave ourselves when out in public."

"There goes my lucky day. But speaking of luck, I wonder how Maazel came by his name. Maazel means luck, I think."

"Yes I'm sure it does when it's spelled with a single `a'. His is doubled up. You know, a stretch version."

"You don't think they just made a mistake when his grandaddy was being processed through immigration on a real busy day?"

"It seems I've read somewhere that things like that used to happen all the time. But should it matter? You're not inclined to think it was his name that made him, are you?"

"You never know."

"Well aren't you the superstitious one? Who'd have thought."

"Like we were getting into, back at the hotel. Could be we're birds of a feather after all."

But Adam thought the question needed further consideration. Maybe with a more providential name, "luck" quite possibly might have entered the scene and come on strongly enough to discourage the Horla from taking him over. There was no letting go of that same stubbornly entrenched conviction about his mental predicament. Rogoff could sound off all he wanted to about having screwed up brain connections. Adam would cling to the idea of being, perhaps, mortally jinxed.

Also he'd been having uneasy feelings that the Horla no longer came and went just willy-nilly. He, or it, was always there, hovering nearby and waiting for opportune moments to intrude and force a perseveration of almost any one of his movements, or for that matter, even his thoughts. At first it looked like this evil spirit had haunted only his home because it was there that most of his almost endless checking took place. That theory had been ditched as soon as he'd realized that some measure of psychological sanctuary could be found in other places only because he had no serious or personal responsibilities there.

But Miranda wasn't buying any far fetched notions about Maazel being simply lucky.

"Ideas like that will get you nowhere. If Maazel is fortunate it's only for having been born a musical genius. You know, a child prodigy. At least that's what I got from the newspaper yesterday. But having one kind of talent doesn't mean he's good at anything else. I'll wager he can't even row a boat."

"So what? Neither can I."

"Or raise money for a political convention."

"Neither can I."

"You were misleading me?"

"No. But I'm out of commission. Remember? I'm on hold, waiting for these damn pills, the Prozac, the wonder drug, to kick in and liberate me, get this monkey off my back, and send him packin'."

"Oh dear. I had no idea it was that bad."

"Now you know."

But could it become worse, he wondered? Seriously worse? Could he find himself paralyzed someday? Not paralyzed in a physical sense but rather not capable of mounting enough surety for anything to initiate either important actions or thoughts. Adam set himself to imagining that kind of fellow, someone like himself, standing in a cluttered room somewhere, immobile, totally unable to shift position in any direction for lack of certainty about who he was, where standing, how dressed, or by what surrounded. As this depressing concept sank in he recalled that business about joking one's diseases and troubles away. He'd take a stab at it and kid around some.

"Well, it ain't no big thing. As you've probably noticed, I'm cool, Miranda. Real cool."

"You call your behavior cool? From my perspective it's more reminding of an imminent derailing."

"Hey that's pretty good. Then better watch out Miranda. This little choochoo could be headin' for the bend."

These little gags seemed to be helping with his edginess so he kept it up.

"No babe. I'm cool. Real cool. But not too hot to handle. Get it?"

"Adam, you're losing it. Behave yourself."

They had reached Washington Circle and about to turn down Virginia Avenue towards the Watergate and Kennedy Center.

"Adam."

The voice from the rear was strong, sounding almost like a bellow. Adam recognized it immediately. It was Don Foster, administrative assistant to Congressman Jim Baxter of Queens.

"Hey Don. How you doin'? Meet Sasha."

"Delighted ma'm. Listen guy. I've been calling you all afternoon. Left three messages. How come you didn't pick up? I take it we're all set for the big dinner in New York next month? Right?"

"Afraid I can't help you with this one, Don. Right now there's too many other things on the fire."

"Jesus, Adam! We were counting on you. Hey now. It's kinda late to be letting us down. Isn't it? We had us a deal. No? After all you've been running this thing every year since the get-go."

Don, an overstuffed and very red faced pol who'd been smiling amiably at first was getting to look quite fractured. After tearing at his neck to loosen his collar and tie, he'd become a little breathless.

Adam was solicitous.

"You okay, old man? Been jogging or just out of shape? Hell. You're drenched. Why you sweatin' like that?"

"Why? Why the hell you think? Shit, Adam. Excuse me, Sasha. It's our big deal annual fund raiser. We took it for sure that you'd be doing it. You're only kidding, right? Say you're kidding Adam, or sure as hell I'm gonna wind up over at George Washington Hospital in the coronary care unit."

"You'd be much better off at Georgetown, Don. Take my word for it old buddy. For emergency care George Washington just plain sucks. Ronnie Reagan was real lucky to get outa there alive."

"Funny. Very funny."

Good, Adam thought. Just what he needed. A few good funny angles being his new meat for countering the Horla.

"Gotta go, Don. Big deal dinner appointment. Look. Give Dick Brown a ring. I betcha he'll have time for you. Come on Sasha, or we're gonna be late."

Miranda could hardly wait until they were a few steps away.

"Why in the world would you ever call me Sasha?"

"It's so much better sounding than Miranda. And I've never known a Miranda so I keep thinking you're maybe some kind of Russian. Let me tell you. I knew one of them kind real well. So is it okay if I call you Sasha from here on in? Besides, it's none of that guy's business who I'm currently datin'."

"Did I hear you say dating?"

"Sure. I'm getting big ideas about us."

"Look here. I'm Miranda, as was my darling mother and her mother before her. And I shall not be relinquishing my name simply because you have problems not only with proper behavior but also it seems with your memory. However, if you'd prefer it, you may call me MJ for short, J being for my middle name Jean."

"Have it your way, MJ, but like I was saying about you and me..."

"Yes?"

He sensed a genuine interest in some kind of a proposition. Thought he could read it in her eyes.

"Hey. Very tricky. Your eyes have stopped bein' hazel. Damned if out here in the light, they've turned all green."

"Nothing's turned, Adam. They've been green forever. But you don't like them that way?"

"Sure I do. I'm just nuts about them along with your whole getup. And I've other ideas. Including how you could come in real handy."

"Press on if you must. But I assure you I've heard it all before and would appreciate being spared one of your little sure fire, I wager, and well worn approaches."

"No, no, Sasha... MJ. You've got it all wrong. Look. You did me a real service back there at the Mayflower. Remember how I was goin' over the tab and searchin' through my wallet? Hell, if you hadn't checked things out for me, you know, reassured me right then and there about not having dropped anything out of it, and telling me that I added up the bill just right... Why, Christ! We could still be there. You are one hell of a find. And also, a peachy looking one. You could even turn out to be my very own and kinda special green-eyed mazel."

"Not a chance, Adam. We are going to a concert. If you behave yourself, we might even get together again someday in the not too distant future. In the meanwhile, just have yourself another pill or next chance you get, lay all this heavy stuff on your shrink. I have neither the time nor the intention of becoming some kind of full-time grand verifier. Dear me. Take a look. There's an absolute mob down there."

Miranda had noticed that even from a two block distance lots of people could be seen converging on the Kennedy Center. Cars were starting to cue up in long lines and having to wait their turn for access to the underground garage. Adam couldn't remember anything like it.

"Whatcha know! Looks like Maazel is gonna be quite a draw. But listen up. You gotta hear me out on this thing. My psychiatrist, his name is Rogoff, is planning to team me up with some gal, someone what's called a behavioral therapist. And she's gonna do no better than what you just did. She's supposed to stay with me when I'm into my worst kind of checking and encourage me to beg off, you know just say no to it all. It's supposed to give me like enough of a morale boost to block or interrupt some kind of a repeating cycle that's carrying on in a deep and malfunctioning part of my brain. Now maybe, and it's only a maybe, between that and the Prozac, I'll get to give my monkey the slip and stage a breakout from the mess I'm in."

At the same time, Adam could just about visualize an unimpressed Horla taking note of what seemed, on the face of it, this rather flimsy, perhaps even ridiculous, countermeasure.

Miranda had been listening a little more attentively than before and appeared to be getting curious.

"Just when does this sort of thing affect you the most?"

"When I lock up at night and when I take off in the morning. It's then that I spend a helluva time staring at my garage doors and making absolutely sure they're down. That can take as long as five, ten minutes. Then I pull on the back door, the yard door, the kitchen door, over and over again. At night it's not unusual for me, in spite of all this, even after I'm finally back inside the house, to go back on out and check those garage doors all over again. I just stand there and stare at them, counting panels, hinges, support chains, springs, anything to convince myself the goddamned doors are truly in their rightful down position."

"Then what?"

"It never works. I never quite get the necessary feeling,

the one that connects with being sure. What my psychiatrist calls closure. Somehow, eventually, I give up on it. I just can't stand doing it even one more time. But then it's just so I can get back inside and start checking other things like the dials on the oven and the stove. I try to make certain the toaster's plugged out, the sink faucets are turned off. Lady. It's murder. Absolute murder. It takes me almost an hour, every damned night, before I ever get to bed."

Attentive or not, Miranda was not about to let any of this get her down.

"Like they say, `everybody oughta have a maid'. That's a song, rather, from a Broadway show as I recall. But look here, Adam. You don't mean to tell me that there are behavioral therapists out there who will hire on to stay overnight, with a strange person like you, do you?"

"Damned if I know. How else could you deal with something like this?"

"Well keep me posted. I find it all quite fascinating. But as I said, you can't count on me for anything of the sort."

Adam nudged her with his elbow.

"Come on. I've got a twelve room house. You can have the whole first floor to yourself."

"I wouldn't think of it. So let us set this whole matter aside at once. Anyhow, where are we going for dinner?"

"Dinner? You only just ate. I thought you were only planning on desert. Wasn't that the deal?"

"Come on Adam. Those sandwiches were no more than hors d'oeuvres. They were precariously slight."

"Okay, okay. Only we're not heading for some dumpy cafeteria. I'll see if we can't get in that fancy place up top. A class act like you rates something real special. And this one's on me."

"Well really. Who would have thought? What are you up to, Adam?"

"I've been dazzled. That's all. Dazzled big time." After leading her through the Kennedy lobby, filled with both tourists and ticketholders for the evening concert, Adam followed Miranda onto an elevator going to the rooftop terrace restaurant. It was jammed, making it necessary to stand on line outside and await table assignment. She resumed her interrogation of him.

"Another thing. What was going on back there between you and that other guy? You know, Don."

"It's a bitch. The truth is, I owe him. I signed on for the job, but what could I say? That I'm unable to follow through because right now my minds all screwed up and I first gotta get myself straightened out? No way. If one word of it got leaked, in my business, I'd be washed up. Better to say I'm busy, real, real busy. Anyway, I've got enough dough put aside to knock off for quite a while. And it isn't that I just need lots of steady time to hang out with this here behavioral therapist Rogoff's gonna set me up with, or that I'm afraid to work while on medication. There's simply no way I can wheel, deal and hustle my way through one of these fundraising things and also be checking, checking, checking. That dog won't hunt."

Adam had been hanging over Miranda's shoulder and speaking in hushed tones, not wanting to air his most intimate concerns and be overheard by anyone else waiting on line.

"What kind of a dog is it?"

Some guy, presumably a sporting type of sorts and standing directly in front of Miranda apparently had a keen enough sense of hearing to have caught the vehement last part of his declaration and was acting as if entitled to clarification.

"What dog?"

"Yours. The one that won't hunt."

"I don't have a dog."

"You're confusing me."

"No. Maybe you're just slipping. Past a certain age it may be unavoidable."

Miranda decided to intercede.

"He was merely employing a figure of speech. It had nothing to do with dogs or hunting. It's an expression intended to mean that some planned thing, if you please, won't fly. It won't work."

Adam, seeing that the maitre d' had signalled a free table, reached past Miranda and tapped the confused one on the chest.

"Hey old buddy, they've got a table for you, so you want to eat or not? But don't get any idea you're gonna dawdle here and get more language lessons from us. Because if you don't nail that table, we will."

The man turned and led his wife away, the two of them looking a bit spooked as in conspicuous haste they headed off behind a waiter. Miranda sensed that something was amiss.

"Look. Aside from all the mental disturbance, you really don't get on very well with people, do you? If I hadn't interceded when I did you would have kept right at it determined to antagonize that poor man. Am I not right? So what is it with you?"

"You're sounding just like my ex. Here's the deal. I've never been able to comprehend why it's up to me to get along with anyone who just happens to come down the pike. That guy was a damned snoop. His business here was with his woman and getting a table, not to eavesdrop on us. And it's the second time today some jackass has sailed up out of nowhere and presumed that I wanted to carry on a conversation with him. The other time was on a bench in Dupont Circle. It's like these guys think there's been something goin' on between us that needs continuin'. You know, like we've been confiding in one another for years, and now we're all set to pick up where we left off. I don't like it one damned bit. Especially now that I've only got eyes and ears for you, kid."

"Thank you. I'm truly flattered by your intentions. But with such an attitude, how in God's name have you ever managed to get along in your line of work?"

"I don't work in God's name or anyone else's. I work in mine alone. And I stay focused. Tend to business. Deal only with particular people with whom it's gonna pay off. The ones who can implement things, deliver the goods. I've got no time for nonproductive chitchat. You think maybe I could sneak in a small kiss? Maybe start things off a little?"

"Thank you but certainly not. Anyway, tell me this: Have you ever considered that perhaps all of your meticulous targeting of other people has become so out of control that it's finally gotten you in your present quandary?"

"Funny. That's what Rogoff was intimating up until I straightened him out real good. Hey. There's a free table. And we're getting the signal. So let's go."

They were assigned a table on the upper level of the restaurant with commanding views of an outside terrace where people were strolling, and where the Potomac river running just below them was being crossed by evening traffic taking the Memorial Bridge to Virginia. Nothing much further was said while they observed the outside scene. Then, passing on drinks or appetizers, they each ordered salads and the catch of the day, rockfish. But when Miranda wasn't looking, Adam sneaked another Prozac. This made his dose for that first day more than had been prescribed but he feared to drink any more scotch and needed something to steel him for what he had in mind. Their order placed he decided to lay it on the line.

"Look. If all this is getting to be more tedious than you bargained for or what my company's worth, just say the word and I'll take off."

"Relax. I find you interesting."

"Yeah, but you were expecting company for a concert, not an up front seat at the freak show."

"You are not a freak. Far from it. Now let's settle down for a pleasant time. Rockfish is my favorite and I'm looking forward to a lovely dinner."

"I admire your appetite."

"And?"

"Everything that comes with it."

"Thank you. That's very sweet."

"But you're not drawn to me. Right? Come on. Say you're not, and we're done with it."

"Don't be impossible, Adam. Whatever is the big rush? I'm drawn to taking you to this concert. Period. Now let any other ideas you might be having take a rest."

For all this boldness any ideas he had along such lines were but fanciful. Whatever Miranda's physical endowments, she, no more than any of the other good looking women of this day had occasioned an arousal.

While she was taking in the view and starting on her salad, Adam picked at his plate wondering when next he'd be put upon by the Horla to check on something. In spite of Rogoff's assurance to the contrary he was hopeful that this extra Prozac would kick in and carry the day for him by preventing it. He gauged himself while sweating out the Horla's next move.

"You got a boyfriend?"

"Not presently. The last one cheated on me and once upon a time there existed a husband. It seems we are members of the same club."

"Gee. Aren't you young for that?"

"That was precisely the point. My husband and I were much too young to get married and he never grew up."

"With me it was opposite. The wife and I became too old to stay married. And any heat still there got used up in never-ending arguments. Know what I mean?"

"I am quite familiar with the scenario."

"You know? I'm thinking tonight's concert could be wrong for people like us maybe needing a little lift. Because old Mahler was so deep into death, redemption, rebirth... all those nasty bits and pieces. And he was on his last legs with cancer when he hit on this one, the ninth. But then again, in my opinion, nothing's ever beautiful, I don't think, unless it's real sad."

"Now why couldn't you have kept all of that to yourself? Really Adam. Anyway, here comes the fish."

"Sorry about that."

His confidences regarding Mahler hadn't taken the edge off her appetite. Even halfway through her plate, she was starting to look into his. But this time he determined to eat. Having taken the extra dose of Prozac, he thought to be better off not having an empty stomach. And so he hastened through his dish just about matching her bite for bite.

"Okay. Now for that desert I was promised. I want the tartuffo."

"What the hell is that?"

"A ball of Italian vanilla ice cream under a chocolate crust."

"We'll make it for two."

It was delicious. And enough so to summon for a second one. Then she really surprised him.

"Look Adam, I know what you said but I insist on paying for all of this. So don't even think of reaching for that horrible old wallet of yours. There'll be nothing at this particular table for you to check on. Let's not spoil this moment. Some other time or place, should your wallet happen to be out, you can pay me back."

Profoundly affected by such consideration he was silent as he watched her draw out a credit card and pay the bill. In a few moments he was waiting in the restaurant foyer while she headed for the ladies room. This was turning out to be an exceptionally sensitive and considerate woman. The sight of her a few minutes later beaming broadly as she strode back in his direction had him in an odd whirl. Out on the terrace they took the promised walk around the building. There was no one else on the elevator when they rode it back down to ground level. Adam passed an arm around her shoulder and bending forward, pressed a tentative kiss upon her forehead. As they stepped through the elevator doorway back into the concert hall lobby, Miranda turned quickly and smiled up at him more broadly than before.

"There Adam. By Jove. I think you've got it. And we are certain to have us an absolutely lovely time."

What Adam had was a lump in his throat and the sense of a tear in his eye.

Her tickets were for two excellent seats in the eighth row. They were center section and on the aisle. He thought it time for a confidence.

"You know, I tend to come on a lot tougher than I actually am."

"Adam, please. Right now, no psychodynamics. Not a word until after the concert. If you want, you can lay another sweet little kiss on my noodle."

He leaned across and complied.

"How's that?"

"I said to shush. It was lovely, just lovely. Now be quiet."

The Mahler ninth would be the only work of the evening. Adam, musically illiterate, was however an audio buff and a collector of records and CDs. He had installed, by his own labors, in an oversized room of his spacious house, multiple panels of tall free standing electrostatic speakers driven by banks of high end amplifiers, sophisticated turntables, CD players, and time delay devices.

From the very inception of that enterprise he had striven to reproduce as much as it was technically possible to do so, cost being no deterrent, orchestral sounds as he might hear them from about the same concert hall position that they occupied this very evening. Generally, after a concert, with the musical sounds still fresh in his mind, he would return home and if need be, tweak his system to higher levels of faithfulness. Moreover, Adam appreciated the emotional effects that music could have on him and had recently developed a somewhat experimental interest in the visual aberrations generated when, and only when, he listened to musical sounds with his eyes closed.

Tonight, however, as the house lights dimmed, Adam's eyes were opened wide for his first glimpse of Maestro Lorin Maazel. He knew that the man was sixty five and yet he seemed so youthful, so athletic, as he moved briskly across the stage, acknowledged the Pittsburgh Symphony concertmaster, and bowed to his audience. His handsome unlined face framed eyes that generated an engaging and knowing warmth. Unlike any other conductor he'd seen before, this one, albeit quite serious in demeanor, was eminently likeable. Orderly, without extraneous movement, he stepped to the podium and faced his orchestra, arms only slightly extended, seemingly afloat, left fingers long and tapering, suspended in a position of delicate flexion, right fingers barely grasping the baton. Intense anticipation pervaded the hall in response to this minimalist but magical presence.

When the first sounds were emitted Adam wasn't sure that Maazel's hands or baton had actually moved or even if he was really hearing anything at all. It was more like being mysteriously reminded of something. But it was soon apparent that something had to have been communicated from conductor to orchestra because there was this distant, mournful, painfully evolving reminiscent melody, barren of hope, a testament to what was irretrievable, beyond all possibility of restitution or atonement. Adam knew this symphony well but had never heard it this way. And an hour later, irrespective of intervening Mahlerian thunder or diversions into tuneful folklore, which repeated that initial theme in artfully transmogrified form, he awaited and was rewarded with the dreadful, languorous, final suggestion of those very first notes.

Final? Actually there was no true end to it. Maazel simply stood there, frozen in place, as if he would never move again, awaiting a last, an ultimate note, a note that was the logical one, the one demanded by finality, and perhaps as softly expressed as it had been sounded at the beginning of this infinitely sad symphony. But it never materialized. It was intended only to be imagined, perfectly imagined, and could not be produced by mere mortals or mechanical instruments. Adam had the feeling that a dying gasp had been only partially exhaled. Death? Life? They were both suspended. Like Maazel himself, suspended before him.

Then the maestro turned slowly and faced them, head bowed, shoulders sagging and remained so while the applause and the cries of "Bravo. Bravo" exploded about him. When at last he raised his head, his face was without expression. Adam thought that the eyes though might now be those of Mahler, a Mahler chastened and beyond all hope.

Maazel took three unsmiling curtain calls and was gone.

Adam turned to Miranda.

"What do you think?"

"It was marvelous but so sad."

"Not the music. The guy, Maazel."

"Very impressive. Soft and yet dynamic."

"Knocked your socks off, hey?"

"I suppose you could put it that way."

They remained seated, waiting for those behind them to arise and file into departing queues. Adam pulled out his copy of the Kennedy Center program guide.

"Did you read this thing?"

"Some of it."

"The part on Maazel?"

"What's this gonna be? A quiz?"

"Nope. It's just so hard to grasp. Here's this guy, conductor, violinist, writer, administrator, composer, you name it. He's conducted over four thousand performances. Recorded hundreds of symphonies and other works. Travels all around the world leading a bunch of orchestras. And the guy, at sixty-five, looks fresh as a daisy and spoiling for more of the same. I also read somewhere that he's got a new wife and two infant kids. How the hell does he do it?"

Miranda did not seem impressed.

"Genes, it's all in the genes."

"Luck huh? The Maazel of the genetic draw. Right?"

"I told you his is with a double a. Luck is with one a."

"Yeah? So he's doubly lucky. That's how I see it. Come on, we can go now."

Walking out, Adam was finding it hard to accept that their arrangement for the evening was just about over.

"Hey girl. I owe yuh. It was a fantastic concert. And don't forget, there's also the tab for dinner. How about a cup of coffee while we settle up?"

"Do I rate one more dessert?"

"Absolutely. Come on. We'll head for the Encore café."

"Lead on, Buster."

They took the elevator to the top of the Center once more and entered the Encore, a cafeteria. It was a pleasant, largely empty place, just across from the terrace restaurant now closed down for the night. After loading up a tray with coffee and apple cobblers, Adam slid it before the checkout cashier, handed her a ten dollar bill from out a side pocket of his jacket, accepted the change, and led Miranda to another table with a quite good view of the

Potomac. It was all executed rather smoothly. He courted her approval.

"How's this?"

"Perfect. Just perfect. But what's with the ten dollar bill in the pocket?"

"Did you want to see me glued to my wallet again, over there, and under that gal's nose? Hardly. I carry ten bucks in every pocket. Saves me from all that business of checking out what's left in the damned wallet after I start messing with it. Look. Do me another one of your neat little favors. Here's the wallet. Draw, I figure something like seventy bucks and then hand it back to me."

"Why don't I just keep the wallet and save you a lot of grief."

"Don't ridicule me."

"I'm sorry."

"That's okay."

Eyeing him curiously she did as suggested. Adam resecured the wallet in a back pocket, pressed upon it a few times to confirm its enclosed, secured, presence and appeared relieved.

"Good. That's over. And we're evened up. But not exactly. I can't really repay you for taking me to hear the symphony. It was mind boggling. So was the band leader."

"'Band leader'? What a putdown. Sounds like you resent him."

"Well in a way, I do. But envy, I guess, is a better word for it. You know how it goes: 'all men are created equal, but some more equal than others'. This guy, like we said, just plain lucked out. I betcha right now, this very moment, old Maazel is hot footing it somewhere in a jet setter kinda whirl with not a worry or thought for checking out anything. And me, I'm his opposite, rooted, bogged down, damned near paralyzed for having to repeat just about everything I do then check it again and again, and again. Christ. I'm stuck, and it's like having my nose shoved down in it."

"You can't know that. The man could be exhausted right now and looking to a good night's rest. I wager he's sitting in his dressing room utterly depleted, no coat, shoes off and ready to bed down in a fancy suite over there in the Watergate Hotel. There's a real possibility that what we saw tonight was total effort for the old boy, a matter of giving it his best shot and now he needs desperately to recuperate. Maybe even, his young wife has been pressing him for more attention than she's been getting and, in spite of his being so fatigued, is about to harp on it again. Meanwhile, there he sits, thinking about family obligations and what in heaven's name is he doing at his age, starting to raise a family?"

"What you wanta bet?"

"Come on, Adam. Let's eat these cobblers. They look like they might be delicious."

For him, the cobbler looked better than it tasted. Too much dough and the apple wasn't tart enough. But he ate it without complaining. Maybe this thing here with Miranda could be the start of some kind of a relationship. So he'd better not be bitching about everything. Especially about things that really didn't matter at all. Like the pastry in a damned cafeteria. After all, she'd been amazingly tolerant so far about all of his griping. Just why was hard to figure. He was starting to wonder about that and also about feeling no effects at all from the third Prozac. At least he was no longer unsure of his dates and of his sense of time. So there was no improvement but no definite adverse side effects either. Miranda looked to be his only countable blessing.

"I'm a real pill, right?"

"No you're a darling, but a sick, sick one."

Christ. She had her shoe on top of his and was rubbing it back and forth. Someone might easily see what was going on beneath their table.

"I wouldn't want anyone to feel sorry for me."

"A tough guy, huh?"

Now she was pressing harder with her foot and kind of swiveling it as well.

"Why are you doing that? You after another cobbler?"

"No. I just figure that soon they're gonna have you cured and then you'll be a blast to be with. So I'm putting out a signal."

She withdrew her foot, sat back and sipped her coffee. In other times such a bold female overture would surely have provoked him considerably. Hard to believe, especially with it coming so unexpectedly and from such a handsome woman, that he was almost numb to her forward gesture.

"Till then, huh?"

"As I've told you, things have a way of playing out. Asking questions hardly ever helps any."

"Well I've got one for you, anyway. What makes you think I'm ever gonna shake the monkey off my back?"

"Why is it a 'monkey'? Your doctor has told you it's simply a disorder. One that's not all that uncommon and for which there is treatment."

"Okay. Call it a devil."

"I don't get it. You insist on making it some kind of a spook. One minute it's a monkey. Next, it's like Satan."

"Because then, maybe I can shake it. If I'm doing these things because I'm just fated, you know, genetically programmed to self destruct, to have certain deep parts of my brain let me down by crapping out at this time of my life, then it's like me bearing witness to my very own premature decomposition. That's a helluva rap. No?"

"But that other stuff, the business about devils and monkeys, is being counterproductive."

"Yeah? Look. I'm still going along with the treatment. I even slipped myself an extra pill tonight, when you weren't looking. But what is my man Rogoff promising me? Maybe, get this, there's no more than a maybe that with medication and the behavioral thing I'll get to feel somewhat better. He suggests as much as sixty per cent better. But that's gotta be with real high doses, much more than I'm presently taking. And no cure. Absolutely no chance for a cure. And when sickies like me stop taking their medicine, they relapse. All of them are right back where they started. How does that grab you? You better not figure on me being any kind of a, like you say, 'blast' in either the near or the distant future. So secretly, well not really so secretly, I'm clinging to the slim hope, some kinda chance of somehow shaking this thing on my own. I tried already to put some of my own ideas into play and I'm toying with another."

"For instance?"

"No, no. Forget it. They're kooky and in a way laughable."

"Try me."

"I'd be embarrassed."

"Come on, Adam."

Now she was kicking him beneath the table.

"Comedy, sex play, and maybe total material deprivation."
She broke out laughing and took awhile to come up
for air.

"I think that's marvelous. You shouldn't be embarrassed, Adam. Anyway, I'd never figure you for that kind
of a person."

"Like I tried to tell you, I hang tougher than I really
am. If I didn't, the political hardasses I have to deal with
would walk all over me."

"So who are you into for gigglies, Whoopi Goldberg?"

"She's too ugly to be funny."

"That's mean."

"All the same I'd prefer Walter Matthau and George
Burns."

"And for that other thing?"

"Right now, there's only you."

"My word, aren't you the conniver? All night long
you're figuring me to be some kind of an antidote to that
monkey of yours? A quick lay for a quick fix, is that it?
Well I never would have guessed."

"Come on, don't get silly. You're nothing like that. It's
just that, far as I can remember, I used to let everything
go to pot once I started getting hooked on someone. But
all it took was anticipation. The heavy stuff wasn't even
necessary. Problem is, like I intimated before, something
else has happened. These days I'm not turning on. Rogoff
says it's because I'm depressed. I tried experimenting with
it on the way downtown this afternoon and it was a dud.
So, so far, it's all academic."

"Good heavens! Now what exactly were you up to
before you started coming on to me? Forget it. I'll use my
imagination. No. It'd be better if you told me."

"Hey. I'm no damned pervert. All I did was ogle some well stacked luscious likelies while I was coming down to the Mayflower."

"And me?"

"Tell the truth?"

"It's a lovely habit."

"I didn't even notice you until you blew all that smoke my way. I was just lookin' in the mirror, feelin' sorry for what I saw there."

"And then?"

"Well it wouldn't take a slow study to see that you're the ultimate knockout."

"But I don't charge your battery either?"

"Nope. Anyway, not so far. Not even with that neat little footsy maneuver of yours. Sad, huh?"

Miranda finished her coffee and stared at him, seemingly perplexed at what to make of it all.

"I'm stymied."

"Tell me about it. How do you think I feel? Only first rate idea I've come up with is for you to be my behavioral therapist. You know? I wasn't kidding. It looks like you have a natural flair for the thing. Like I said, you could take over the whole first floor at my place and anything else you wanted. There's an extra car in the garage. I'll buy whatever else you need. You wouldn't even have to give up your apartment. I'll see to that too and..."

"Adam. Leave off of it. I've had lots of propositions but this one tops them all. You're about to drive me batty, too. I am not moving in with you. It is out of the question. I only just met you. I have a very responsible position. I cannot be your nursemaid or whatever else you are contemplating it will take to make you better."

"Thanks a lot. Talk about being mean."

"We were better off discussing Maazel."

"Who is one lucky son of a bitch."

Miranda appreciated the respite from the other subject and went with it.

"Ever stop to think that the man might have a very narrow existence? So music is his life. So what? There are people like him who are no good at all for anything else. They don't read. Can't add. Wind up completely self centered in a world of their own. And so catered to they have no self reliance to fall back on in a real pinch."

"Baloney. The guy's flat out drunk on digging life through music and so what if it's to the exclusion of everything else? That's all any reasonable person can hope for. A totally exclusionary diversion that blots out all of the shit and the pain and the sorrow and even distorts what death is all about. Like he just pulled off tonight, with his Mahler kick."

"Adam, I'm starting to get real tired. Let's go."

"Okay. I'll cab you home."

"It's not necessary."

"It is. I need to know where you live. Suppose I have to reach you in an emergency."

"Like?"

"Like checking me out. And making sure I'm still breathing."

Five

Miranda made Adam stay in the cab, insisting that she make it to her door alone. She gave him two phone numbers and accepted an appreciative peck on the forehead. Then Adam continued on home.

It was not something to look forward to. His tedious day was over but home was where the Horla had him in full fetters.

Entry was either by front door key or electronic operation of his garage doors. Since the front door was secured by chain and dead bolt he had to take return access through the garage. Once inside he could operate a switch to run back down whichever door had been raised for making entry. That was when the Horla insisted on his kind of proof regarding closure. Not Rogoff's kind which had something to do with the workings of Adam's brain but a mechanical kind which was concerned with the arrangement of ordinary nuts and bolts of a door that was presumably at rest in a down position. The problem was the Horla had never divulged to Adam how that mechanical proof was to be arrived at. That being the case, and there being no science for it either, he could only resort to simple trial and error. Endless trial and error. This exercise in futility was carried out in several ways, all of them needing to be repeated an unpredictable number of times.

First off, the door that had been raised and lowered was stared at. He would reason with himself that if by some unimaginable phenomenon, it had not in all truth been lowered, or if by dint of some kind of unaccountable action, the electric door operator, without intervention by him, had malfunctioned and raised the door once more, he should be having a clear view of the driveway outside. Which was not the case. But which, nonetheless, was never surely, inarguably, never the case necessitating that he take another tack and compare the door that had been raised to the other one, the one which hadn't . Then, if hinges, lever arms, panes, the crossbars of both, seemed to be in identical and parallel positions, some modicum of reassurance, might reasonably be taken regarding the final resting location of that door which had been utilized for taking entry.

The problem was that reason could have no sway in any of this. Only exhaustion, embarrassment, an intolerable level of sadness, and finally, some vague notion that if he had repeated all of this business so many times, Christ. chances were, or at least there was some modicum of possibility it must have been done right. Must? Never must. At best it was a possibility.

And so, even after he left the garage, passed through a vestibule and another door which led into the house proper, and the kitchen, and had closed it behind him, residual uncertainty, the heart of his undeniable compulsion, dictated the necessity to go back out again, to stare once more, and line up everything another time. This went on and on until finally he had an inkling, by virtue of sheer exhaustion but never by true certitude, that his obligation to secure the garage had been met.

Then there followed much pulling against the latch of the inner house door until it seemed to be secure enough for him to enter the back kitchen. Later on, before going up to bed, he had his prescribed rituals for that place also. There were light switches and gas burner controls to be pressed upon and twisted to an extent he sometimes feared would wrench them from their very sockets.

On this and every other night his final task, after all of these odious time consuming activities had been completed, was to set the burglar alarm. Set. Check. Turn off. Set. Check. Turn off. Set. Of course, no matter how much he stared at the illuminated control panel, whether or not he'd coded the thing properly was as always, in the end, up for grabs.

Well, if ever the worst came to the worst, there were always his guns.

He did not sleep well that night or on those which followed, and assumed after rereading the drug warning given him by the pharmacist that this difficulty represented a side effect of the Prozac. As for other changes in his behavior, he couldn't pin them down. Euphoria or disorientation did not recur and his compulsivity continued unabated. This was so much so that he remained at home the entire weekend, taking his medication, watching TV, and listening to Mahler CDs including a rehearing of the ninth, one recorded by Von Karajan. To not leave the house was deliberate. As long as he stayed holed up, there was little need to go through the compulsory rituals involved in going and coming. Although his supply of groceries was starting to run low, Adam decided to make do, at least for awhile, with what he had. Going out to shop or even to open the front door for pizza or other kinds of home delivery, had become out of the question. It would involve too much additional checking.

On several occasions he dialed Miranda's number but got no answer. Then, on Sunday night, he decided to call Rogoff at home. His doctor picked up on the first ring.

"Hello?"

"Hey. You got any idea how bad this is?"

"Adam. Right?"

"Who else? All your other patients are doing hunky-dory. Correct?"

"Not necessarily. But they are generally polite and exercise at least a modicum of self restraint. So I would have no difficulty whatever in making the necessary distinction."

Adam paid no mind to Rogoff's putdown.

"I even tried recruitin' my own behavioral therapist but the chick wanted no part of the deal."

"You're supposed to call my office for that referral. Are you consulting with someone else now?"

"Not really. It was a woman I met in a bar."

"A bar?"

"What's the matter? We got a bad connection or don't you screw in your hearing aid when you're at home?"

"Unfortunately, I'm getting all of this quite well."

"It was a gal who took to it real natural like. At least, that's how it seemed to me. She eased me out of one of my checking routines like she knew all about it. Otherwise, I might still be sitting there, goin' through my wallet. But she is otherwise employed. You want to round someone up and send them over?"

"You mean now? at seven o'clock on Sunday night? You're not serious."

"These days, I'm only serious. I have no inclination, whatever, to kid around. The whole situation is getting to be serious, real, real, heavy kind of serious. Pretty soon they're gonna find me doin' nothing but sitting here and contemplating my navel."

"Whatever you may have read, Adam, that is not part of the syndrome."

"Come on, be a good guy and bail me out."

"Tomorrow, Adam. Like we told you, 'tomorrow'. That's when you're supposed to call the office and please think twice about phoning me at home unless you are having a real emergency."

"What's the matter? You watching baseball or somethin'?"

Rogoff hung up.

Adam dialed Miranda again. This time she answered.

"Good. I was beginning to think you gave me a bum steer with the numbers."

"Adam?"

"Why is it that everyone asks if it's me before I ever announce myself? Just don't hang up on me like the last guy."

"Who was that?"

"Rogoff, the psychiatrist."

"Were you being polite?"

"Well..."

"Adam, you get more flies with honey than..."

"Sweetheart, with honey, in my experience, you get cockroaches."

"No doubt about it, Adam. You do have a way. Okay, why are you calling me?"

"I think Rogoff was watching baseball. You watching baseball too?"

"No."

"Good. Then you won't hang up on me."

"Keep this up and I'll find a better reason."

"I just need to talk to someone. I've been locked in here since I dropped you off Friday night."

"Is that good for you? I thought that's where you have most of your problem."

"Right. But I couldn't handle the goin' and the comin' thing. How about keeping me company for awhile?"

"When?"

"Like now. You could check yourself in and out. I might trust you to do it correctly."

"Sorry. Tonight I've got to wash my hair."

"Do it over here. There's lots of hot water."

"If you want to talk, talk now."

"That is so cold and impersonal.

"I think I'm feeling worse."

"How so?"

"More and more it's getting to me that maybe something drastic is called for. Even if Rogoff sends someone over to stare at the garage doors and the stove burners alongside me, what's the point? I know, for sure, that as long as they are there, giving me encouragement to break away, I'm probably gonna do it. But I'll just be humoring them and maybe counting on them, like it was with you, to do what I consider to be my dirty work for me. Then, once they're gone, what's the difference? He says that somehow my going through the motions like that is supposed to start up a kinda chemical reaction in my brain that will continue to recycle itself. Kick in with what he calls a serotonin like substance which does the same thing as the Prozac, the difference being it might be more lasting. Still at best, there's only that same damned sixty per cent improvement business to look forward to and like with everything else I may have to stick with all of it forever. I'm still for giving it a whirl, and the Prozac too, but I just know I'm gonna have to come up with something else. Something stronger."

"Like what?"

"Well I'm not gonna burn the damned house down. If that's what you're thinking."

"What a relief."

"Anyway, checking on things is only the tip of what's bugging me. My mind is locked into all kinds of thoughts and ideas that seem to have a life of their own."

"Adam, all of this is quite over my head. These are things you should be discussing with your psychiatrist, not me."

"Yeah, but he hung up on me."

"That does not make me the logical alternative. Have you stopped for one minute to think about how peculiar all of this is? I, a complete stranger, come along and within minutes, before you barely have time to draw a breath, you are spilling what should be your most intimate secrets and troubles."

"You encouraged me. Remember? Said you were the ultimate listener."

"I take it back."

"No way. You dump me now and I'll really be impelled to do something nutty."

"'Drastic', 'stronger', 'nutty'. Anything else on the agenda?"

"I wish I knew. Don't even know what I'm saying, and don't know what I mean half the time when I get this exasperated. But what I was starting to get into is that maybe all this checking is the least part of it all. Thoughts, ideas, intentions, things I merely hear or think about once, a single time, and especially worries, take me over, absolutely take me over. I chew on them and they chew on me, vying for prime time in my head. I don't get to shake off any of it. They line up, go 'round and 'round. No end to any of them, no matter how trivial. That is until I make some kind of a move on them. And that works only partially. Then there are like echoes of sounds I hear which repeat and repeat until they kind of wear themselves out. I'm embarrassed to tell you that I've also started to make little noises, like squeaks or grunts, and small twitches, which I'm able I think, so far, to conceal. You didn't notice me doing any of that, did you?"

"No."

"Scary, huh?"

"I have to admit. You are starting to get to me."

"One other thing. And this is real important. It's not a monkey, or a devil. It's what I call the Horla. Which happens to be either my own representation for what's happening or possibly a better explanation than this brain dysfunction theory Rogoff keeps laying on me."

"What in God's name is a Horla?"

"He doesn't operate in God's name. He's from somewhere else."

Adam gave Miranda a lengthy descriptive account of the Horla, its past, present, and speculative portent for the future. A portent based upon the fatal ending in de Maupassant's story.

"You're telling me some twit in a book tried to kill this thing by burning his own house down?"

"Yeah, but it didn't work. That's why I said I wouldn't do it."

"If you're thinking I'm relieved, forget it. I'm not. My friend you need help. Big time help."

"So you coming over?"

"That's not what I mean. Maybe right now you should be hospitalized."

"Like committed?"

"Well, no. Voluntary."

"No way. Here's where the problem is. Here is where I face up to it. It'd just be better if there were someone else around. Especially an understanding person like yourself."

"Haven't you got any relatives who could come in?"

"None I can stand. Or any, for that matter, who can stand me. My first cousin lives just up the street and we haven't spoken in ten years."

"What a pity."

"So how about it?"

"Knock it off, Adam. It's out of the question. Take your medicine like a good boy. Keep seeing Rogoff. Follow his recommendations and try to cool it."

"All very easy to say."

"Look, I'll call you tomorrow from work. Get some sleep. Good night Adam."

Well it was something. At least there was someone out there interested enough to maybe call up and check on him.

Or to promise to. As for sleeping, the Prozac appeared to be putting an end to it. The only other new thing he'd noticed was that he was beginning to feel a little jittery and perhaps there was a tendency for his lower jaw to kind of quiver or tremble when he didn't close it tightly enough. That was besides the funny little movements and the involuntary noises he'd just described to Miranda. Tonight, though, he'd take a sleeping pill. There were some his wife had left behind in her haste to clear out of the place. So he watched television for a couple of hours, took a pill, and managed to get about five hours rest.

He dreamed that the city had sent workmen out to his house and before he could stop them they had ripped up the garage, the driveway, and laid down fresh macadam. Departing, they insisted he not drive out across the new surface for at least forty eight hours. Ordinarily, a high powered guy like Adam would be having a fit over such involuntary confinement. Now the prospect was not all that bothersome. His dream, in fact, was kind of comforting.

Six

While Adam was taking his morning coffee, the phone rang.

"My name is Louis Reynolds. Is this Adam?"

"Forget it."

And he hung up.

It rang again.

"May I please speak to Adam?"

"No."

There was another ring.

"Look buddy, whatever you're sellin', I'm not buyin'."

"Don't hang up. Doctor Rogoff asked me to call you. I'm a clinical psychologist specializing in behavioral therapy."

"But I was supposed to call him for a name."

"He ran into me this morning and thought it more convenient."

"I understood it'd be a woman."

"Any reason for the preference?"

"You kidding?"

"Well that's encouraging. You've still got your sense of humor. Haven't you?"

"Well rooty, toot, toot."

"How about coming over to the office this morning? We have some time to get you oriented."

"Who says I'm disoriented? Besides which, here is where the battlefield is situated."

"I mean, to familiarize you with the technique. We generally start off with that over here."

"Look. Rogoff's already explained it to me. It's like a buddy system, I guess, even though I had the idea it'd work out boy-girl, not homosexually."

"But you are a card. Aren't you."

"Yeah. I'm an absolute scream. Want to hear me?"

The man ignored his offering and pressed on.

"What exactly is the problem? Compulsive hand washing for instance?"

"I never wash, bathe, shower. Sometimes I have to force myself to use toilet paper, but not all that often. Look. Joking aside, didn't Rogoff fill you in at all?"

"There wasn't that much time."

"I'm what he calls a checker. It's very depressing."

"That's great. Sorry, I didn't quite mean that. It's just that I've done very well with such patients. How long has all of this been going on?"

"This time, for several months. Last time, it was mild and years ago."

"Are you on medication? Prozac?"

"Rogoff prescribed it on Friday."

"Well good. Let's just see when we can start you."

There was a pause for several minutes until Reynolds came back on.

"How about my stopping by a week from today at ten AM?"

"How about not bothering? How about me just lining up someone else? You crazy, man? You the sick one? Or is it still supposed to be me? Look. I'm not waiting any God damned week to get started!"

"Well, I suppose I could come by today during my lunch hour."

"Good. Bring a couple of bagels. I've still got some lox and cream cheese. I'll be waiting for you."

At noon exactly, Louis Reynolds appeared at Adam's front door. He was a smallish man with close cropped hair, tidily dressed, rather thin, wearing a brown Harris tweed jacket and loafers. His conservative bow tie had obviously been done by hand, meticulously, perfectly. Compulsively? Reynolds face was indifferently sculpted to the point of being eminently forgettable. Adam could not help but wonder if somehow they weren't cut from the same obsessive-compulsive cloth. He led him into the den. Reynolds had come empty-handed, apparently intent only on working. So there'd be no bagels.

"Marvelous home you have here. I'm really delighted to meet you."

Adam continued to do his number on him.

"Why? Business slow? Need more experience? Doin' some kind of a research project on guys like me?"

"None of the above. I just enjoy helping people. So let's get started. Shall we sit right here?"

"Why not?"

"I'll take that as a yes. Now, although the plan calls for me to be present during some of your efforts, and in that role to be what we call a helper, it's important that first I ask you several questions in order to determine if your problem is primarily one of obsessions or compulsions or perhaps a mix. In other words, to classify and grade the severity of the disorder."

"Shoot."

Reynolds then queried Adam as to what his symptoms were, the degree to which he could resist or avoid them, their frequency, and the extent of their compromise of his usual personal and professional activities. Something he identified as the Yale-Brown Obsessive Compulsive Scale.

Having summed up Adam's graded responses to more than fifty questions, he looked up from his notes and appeared ready for some kind of pronouncement. Adam did not find it particularly revealing.

"It's a mix. And a moderately severe one at that. You can not overcome it on your own. You will require help through therapy."

"What else is new? Why would I hole up like this unless I needed help?"

Reynolds had apparently opted to ignore questions he deemed inappropriate.

"Now the second order of business is for you to understand that my role is not only that of support but also to be instructive about the principles of treatment. For example, it is counter productive to attempt control, at the very outset, of the worst of your compulsions. We, or rather, *you*, must start with those things you are drawn to do which are the least troublesome. Progress has to be gradual. Coping with, then overcoming the minor compulsions will so to speak empower you in your final attack upon the more severe rituals of behavior. Gradually, in other words, you will draw the courage to perform better and better by virtue of getting used to being in the line of lesser fire."

"Gotcha."

"Now tell me, in that respect, about some minor thing, perhaps a trivial habit, that you would like to control."

"Zero. The bottom line is that I know damned well, for absolute certitude, that across the board, none of the things I get stuck doing or staring at are worth more than a mere touch, a glance, but I've made every damned one of them a big, big, and time consuming deal."

Reynolds was not to be denied.

"Try. Tell me. 'Fess up. Out with it. Let go with the very first thing that comes to mind."

Adam decided to humor the guy. After all, everyone had a right to try and make a living. So he came up with what could be a real no brainer.

"My wallet. I'm always fingering it to be sure it's still there."

"Excellent."

Reynolds had to be putting him on.

"What's excellent about it? And how minor is it? Someone steals my wallet and they've copped my fucking life. Credit cards, cash, drivers license, important numbers, addresses. They're all there."

"That's not the point. The point is that you came up with it so quickly. It was the very first thing that came to mind. Therefore it will be the compulsion we shall target first."

"Okay. Lay down a barrage. Kill off the mother..."

"No. No. This is something for you to do. Remember I'm only your helper."

"Right."

"Where do you keep your wallet?"

"In my right rear pants pocket."

"Okay. Stand up. Take it out. Throw it on the floor.

Then leave the room. Return and retrieve it, but when you do, drop it back in that same rear pocket without in any way making sure you've really done it."

Adam did as instructed.

"How do you feel?"

"Terrible. I'm dying to at least wiggle my ass and try to feel for it."

"Don't. You must resist. After awhile the tension will pass."

"Says you."

"Trust me."

"I'd rather wiggle my rear end."

"I understand that, but don't do it. If we go on to talk about other things, it will subside."

"I can't think or deal with any other thing. First things come first."

"Resist. Resist."

"Hey. Anyone ever tell you a compulsion is something you just can't not do?"

"It isn't so. The point is that with therapy it can be overcome."

"Yeah? I've wiggled my ass."

"A temporary setback. And not a problem."

"And now I want to put my hand back there to check it out some more."

"Don't do it. We are going to repeat what we just did. Reach back and throw the wallet on the floor again."

"Hell. Won't that be feeling for it?"

"No. You will be doing it at my direction and not in response to your own needs."

"Give me a break. Will yuh? None of this makes any sense."

"Just do it and try to trust me. I know what I'm doing."

Adam complied once more after fairly hurling the wallet to the floor.

"Better?"

"The same. I wanta twitch my ass."

"You mustn't."

"Try and stop me. Save me from myself."

"No sir. That is not my role in this. It has to be accomplished by you. Like I said before, my job is one of direction and support. And why is it that you act as if this is some kind of a joke?"

"It's a way of holding on to what little is left of my sanity. And don't you think this might just be the ultimate mad scene?"

"Absolutely not. Solidly rooted scientific principles are coming into play here, right under your very nose."

"You could have fooled me. And let me remind you, the problem isn't anywhere near my nose. It's adjacent my rear end, which like I keep telling you is right now driving me bonkers. Maybe if you took a feel of it I'd be accepting of my wallet really and truly being back there."

"Not allowed. It's out of the question."

"Even if I promise not to accuse you of coming on to me?"

"Really."

"No use. I just twitched my rear end."

"Adam. It may be you aren't sufficiently motivated."

That did it. Here he was, a just about washed up well known political consultant, driven to desperation and to walling himself off from the world so as to join his Horla in a frantic struggle, if need be to the bitter end, and this dainty little guy, who'd probably never faced up to anything more threatening than a pencil sharpener, was starting to question his motivation.

"That's ridiculous. What do I have to do? Lock myself in the basement without food or water? Take an overdose of something? Then you'd be convinced?"

Reynolds looked apprehensive.

"Hey. You mustn't even think about things like that."

"Man. You are now gonna' tell me what or what not to think? Christ. That's another of my God damned problems. I don't have any more control over my thoughts than over my actions."

"No, no, Adam. We beg to differ. According to our Yale Brown survey you are much more compulsive than you are obsessional."

"Big deal. He'll be glad to hear that."

"Who's that? Doctor Rogoff?"

Adam had let it slip. He had meant his Horla, who had to be right there, and taking in all of this.

"Yeah sure. Doctor Rogoff. Who else? Look. Why don't you and I call a truce on this wallet thing? I'll just practice your little routine on my own and by the time we get together again I'll maybe have worn it out pitching it against every damned floor, and if you want, I'll even bounce it off the walls in this big barn of mine. But while you're here, how about us both going on out back so you can be sizing up my garage doors? Maybe we'll even run them up and down a couple of times while you lay one of your little 'just say no' hexes on me. Who knows? It might just work."

"No, Adam. We mustn't do that."

"Why the hell not?"

"Remember? We start with the little things and work our way up. And don't get the idea I'm some kind of a conjuror who can cast a spell and send you on your well healed way. This is something that takes work, hard long work, and it'll be primarily on your shoulders."

"Okay. What do we do next?"

Reynolds looked at his watch. It was one o'clock. He pulled a small appointment book from a breast pocket, looked at his watch once more, and arose abruptly from his chair.

"Right now, I must be going. Don't want to be late for my one thirty. So, Adam. How about Wednesday at two pm? Okay with you?"

"I'll be here with bells on."

"I like that. Keep it up. God. But isn't humor a saving grace? A blessing? You are on the right track now, Adam. Just stick with the wallet."

"I won't let it out of my sight. It might even wind up being my one and only compulsion. Then we'll polish it off together. Right?"

"Not quite, Adam. But mark my words. After awhile you'll get the hang of all this. 'Bye now."

"So long. And next time don't forget my bagels."

Adam let him out, not sure which of them was the bigger nut all the while hoping, if he was to get some kind of a "hang" out of this, it wouldn't be like he was drawn once more to remember the guy found hanging by his neck in his own clothes closet. No doubt about it. The Horla was the ultimate downer.

As for next Wednesday, he had big, big doubts. It didn't seem like behavioral therapy was a promising way to go. At least it didn't seem so, either by its described method. which he'd been trying to understand, or from this brief experience with it. Problem was, other than the Prozac, there seemed no other way out. Maybe Rogoff. That was if somehow he could get the old guy's undivided attention.

Seven

He had advanced his appointment with Rogoff to Tuesday morning and allowed himself enough time beforehand to pick up groceries and drop off his laundry. Pretty soon he'd also have to stop by his office.

Rogoff seemed to be more outgoing, even empathetic. This did not escape Adam's notice but his own mien was unaffected by Rogoff's new demeanor.

"You taking pills, also?"

This unlimited capacity of his for engendering hostility could at times get oppressive. On the face of it, special awards were probably due his newly solicitous psychiatrist, who chose, in the best professional manner, to ignore his sniping question. For which Adam was secretly grateful. What was to be gained by perpetually popping off at the only person who might know enough to help him? Especially now, when Rogoff was looking to be his best and last resort. As to why he inclined to do his belligerent thing, he hadn't a clue.

"How did it go? Get along okay with Reynolds?"

"We got along just fine. But the way I see it, we don't

move along, and it seems to me, we're not going to. I have a feeling that whole approach is a big joke. And you gotta admit, when it comes to joking around, you're looking at an expert."

"Come on Adam, you don't mean to tell me you're ready to give up after no more than a single session, do you?"

"Who said I'm giving up? Maybe kidding around like that is the only way to deal with this mess I'm in."

"What do you mean, 'kidding around'?"

Adam described his previous day's session with Reynolds.

"Hey doc. Think about it. Tearing through the house and tossin' my wallet every which way and then some, is it the ultimate scream or isn't it?"

"I can't believe you're being truly honest about what Doctor Reynolds was trying to accomplish."

"Doctor?"

"Sure. He's got his Ph.D. And he's one of the better ones in his field."

"Why didn't you get me the very best? I can afford it."

"You were in a hurry. Remember? Anyway, Reynolds will fill the bill nicely if you give him half a chance."

"How can anyone fill the bill who doesn't center on what I'm telling him? Neither one of you guys seems to get it that even when I do hold back from checking on something, there's all the same this damned irresistible urge to cave. I've simply gotta do it. Which is actually worse than how I feel when the Horla dupes me into obliging him over and over again."

"Still with the Horla? Come on. Grow up."

Adam paid no mind to Rogoff debunking of his own concept of what was happening to him.

"Also, how come no one's saying anything about the fact that when I give in and accommodate the Horla, no matter how many times I do whatever he is insisting on, the last time is no more satisfying to me than the first?"

"Look, Adam, all I can say is that if you bear with all of this, a combination of medication and therapy will eventually provide you with a worthwhile moderation of both your compulsive habits and your symptoms. I can only reiterate that approximately sixty per cent improvement is what's generally been reported. When you say that these unfulfilled feelings never leave you it is a reflection upon what we clinicians call a lack of the sense of closure, of the finality of what you do or observe."

"Where does all of that fancy talk leave me?"

"I'm just trying to make you understand that certain parts of the brain are delegated the function of confirming that an event has actually taken place and of conveying a particular and appropriate associated feeling tone. A feeling tone which is needed to reinforce what you might simplistically consider to be a quite automatic recognition that what has transpired, has in fact actually done so. It is a lot more complex than that."

"And that part of my brain is out of order."

"Correct. But understand that when you do things over and over again it's just a perfectly normal mechanism that unfortunately has gone awry. It is no longer inhibited. If we hadn't evolved this wonderfully engineered talent for repeating the things we do to the point of making them automatic, we'd never have walked or run or played the violin. You name it."

"So it's just that a real neat part of my squash has

been sort of unleashed. And I'm unable to tell when it's repeating itself unnecessarily. Right?"

"One could put it that way."

"Well I feel much better. I wouldn't want to buck old Darwin or frustrate evolution. I'll just muddle on and maybe even bust out with pride to be no more, no less, than a shining example of a screwed up variant of what humanity needs for makin' it and to boot, a kind of mind boggling window on our innermost workings."

"You have a way of veering off in the wrong direction when reaching for answers."

"I go off the deep end. Right?"

"And are prone to absolutely uncalled for exaggerations."

"What is this? Put down time at Herr Doktor Rogoff's?"

"Not at all. We'd just like you to get realistic and face up to what's needed to get you over these difficult times. Now I take it there have been no particular side effects from the Prozac?"

"Wrong. I have trouble sleeping and there is a kind of tremor in my jaw, maybe also in my hands and feet. Twice, I had to take sleeping pills. I'd have to say that in general I'm a bit jittery. In fact, I had to make little squeaks or grunts a couple of times. Also, there's some question about my getting high on the first dose and maybe a little confused after I had a drink with the second. But I'm not drinking anymore."

"Well with Prozac it's better to stay off the alcohol. Anyway, alcohol would only tend to make you more depressed. After awhile, particularly when we up the dose, you may require a tranquilizer. I think I've already told you that some patients say they feel 'wired' on this kind of a drug. I'm not sure why you made those little noises. Unless it's a sign of Tourette's syndrome which is occasionally associated with obsessive-compulsive disorder."

"Any idea why I can't bear to get out of bed in the morning? Hell. I'm used to being on my way by six-thirty."

"Depression, Adam. Sooner or later it's bound to ease off as the Prozac starts to work. But like I've been telling you, it's going to take at least another week or two. Don't worry about the other things. They are all par for the course."

Adam thought Rogoff had merely paused but it was taking him much too long to start up again.

"Whatcha dreaming about over there? 'Par for the course' remind you of bein' late for the links or something?"

"No. It's just that I think we've covered all we need to in order to reassure you."

"So I'm dismissed?"

"Have it any way you want. I'd just say we've done what has to be done for the moment."

Adam decided to head for his office and pick up any messages that might be there. Passing by the drugstore on the opposite corner he chanced to think about going inside and seeing if his behind the counter expert on Prozac might pick up on any obvious changes in him. No point to it. He was now inclined to accept Rogoff's insistence of it being much too early for something like that.

That unformulated vagary he'd aired with Miranda about drastic measures being needed stayed with him irrespective of everything said by Rogoff. Whatever course his doctor had set for him, it could still be that something more, something truly drastic, would eventually be called for. Or, if "drastic" was somewhat off the mark, in line with his original thinking on first leaving Rogoff's office, why not pursue a few independent measures of his own? What harm could there be in a multi-pronged attack on the Horla? And if harm did come of it, so what? Ultimately the way things were going he looked to be expendable anyway, so why not take the Horla down also?

Eight

His I Street office was little more than two desks, a few chairs, and two answering machines. Adam had tried several times, over the years, to retain an assistant or a secretary, but when they all quit in a matter of weeks, he'd finally given up on it. If hard-pressed he hired temporaries. He was inclined to think, anyway, that it was more conducive to his ways of doing business if he were not in a position of having to share his political strategies with anyone or run the risk of unsuspected leaks with regard to his various maneuverings. Besides which, this present setup permitted him long stretches of solitary time for hatching his schemes. He could put his feet up, lean back, and chain smoke the illegal Havanas he'd been hoarding for years. The cigars were kept in several carefully maintained oversized humidors.

Today, he was gratified to find that there were only a few telephone messages and none requiring an immediate callback. He considered the wisdom of redictating his outgoing message to let callers know how to reach him on his home number but then remembered it was feasible to access these new fangled machines remotely. In fact, he'd even done it a few times already. Why hadn't he recalled that? Damn it. He'd even had his mail redirected to his home. So there had been absolutely no need for him to trek all the way over here from Rogoff's just for the sake of his telephones. Prozac again? Or should he start to look for early signs of still another kind of mental deterioration? He lit up a Romeo and Juliet half corona and started to cogitate. But what was there to think about? Tomorrow's impending session with Reynolds? Which compulsion might next be targeted? Or must he stick with the wallet routine? After all, he was still nudging it after every throwdown. But better not to consider something else just yet. Reynolds insisted on spontaneity in the selection of troublesome behaviors for modification so he'd not jump the gun. He'd wait until Reynolds and he were together.

And what about Miranda? A gorgeous gal like that, smart too, and all he could think of doing with her was bring her home to serve as some kind of a crutch, a support against his pernicious habits. He'd better stay clear of pondering that one. If his mind had really taken a crazy, sordid kind of a twist, that preposterous brainstorm was too telling a suggestion of it having happened. To dwell on it any further would be much too unsettling.

So back to his special agenda, the matter of somehow opening up another front in the campaign against the Horla. Apparently, comedy or sex play were no longer in the running. And to divest himself of every bloody thing he owned hardly appeared practical, even if in the De Maupassant tale that nutty guy had moved against his Horla by burning his entire house down. But Adam had only joked about doing something like that. He liked his home too much to consider it. Anyway, in the book, burning the house down didn't work. That particular Horla was made of sturdy stuff. Apparently, nonflammable stuff. Adam was far from being pushed to such an extreme. At least for now, misery seemed better than either deprivation or nothingness.

All of this deliberation was getting him nowhere. He reached for a copy of the *Times*. It was last week's. Any news that old was too stale to hold his interest. So by a bad night's sleep, his morning dose of Prozac, and with the hot sun playing upon the back of his chair and neck, he had little recourse but to fall asleep. He dozed for more than an hour never even feeling it when the cigar slipped from his hand and burned a hole in his trouser leg.

"God damn." On awakening to a view of the damage.

He was still sleepy but there was no point in any further catnapping of this kind. It had already managed to give him a crick at the back of his neck and a ruined pair of pants. He'd head for home and siesta properly. Shortly, he locked up, pulled on the office door seven times (a favored number), and went downstairs to hail a cab for home.

The house was dead quiet and conducive to what seemed a pressing need for more sleep. During the ride home he had become even more lethargic. Tired or not he dragged himself through his checking procedure, got himself upstairs, undressed and under the covers, wondering for a few moments what role Prozac might be playing in his drowsiness, which it wasn't supposed to do, until once again he was asleep, this time very deeply.

He awakened, late in the day, refreshed. It was five thirty and he was hungry. No point in dressing. Robe and slippers were all he needed. He was entertaining the idea of a ham sandwich as he took to the stairs.

Half way down, a sixth sense told him that something was dreadfully wrong. After all, he had lived in this old building for so many years he sometimes wondered if the two of them were not on speaking terms. Descending the rest of the way and turning the stairwell corner, such odd-ball ideas gave quick way to a real and startling revelation.

The front hall could no longer boast its handsome antique casement window. In its place there was only a huge rough edged hole which had been battered through the wall. Broken glass and pieces of avulsed hundred-year-old wood were strewn across the floor. A fine oriental vase that usually rested upon the window sill lay in fragments on a rug beneath the offending hole.

He turned left to enter the den. Usually an orderly place for his TV, answering machine, cellular phone, spare watches, VCR, camera, binoculars, intercom, portable radio, and various odds and ends, it was now a shambles, utter chaos. And gone. All of that stuff was gone. He'd been ripped off. Arm chairs and couch lay toppled on their back sides. Important personal papers were strewn across the floor. His attaché case and two small travel bags had also evaporated.

Adam looked about the place further. In the living room several windows had their glass panes shattered during obviously futile efforts to reach the latches. But he'd had them padlocked before this as a precaution. Inside the enclosed porch, the same kind of damage. Obviously, multiple attempts had been made to break in before the ultimate violence had permitted an inordinately crude entry into his front hall. Expensive gortex jackets were also missing from where he had hung them on a clothes tree adjacent the dining room. Bastards. Those were excellent jackets. Favored and expensive jackets.

What a mess to clean up, and then to put back in reasonable order. Christ. How could such a thing have happened in broad daylight and with him at home no less? And how could he have slept through all of this? And why if they knew he was home, how could they be so brazen, so sure he'd stay put, do nothing? And God damn it. He'd not had a chance to get off even a single shot at the bastards. To at least wound? Hell no. To kill all of the sons a' bitches.

He reached for the phone and dialed 911.

"My home's been busted into."

A female officer assured him that a response car would be there as soon as possible. But Adam had already judged that the cops would not be of much help. What he needed mostly was a window repair company. So he drew a number from the Yellow Pages and called. In about twenty minutes there were three Salvadoran guys in a big truck rolling up his front driveway. They were to beat the cops by at least ten minutes. The Salvadorans were straight out of Brooklyn.

"Man. Dey sure did a job on you. But we seen woise. Last place we wuz at, before dey busted de window out, dey tried hackin' der way tru de fuckin roof."

Adam drew little consolation from this advisement. All he wanted now was to get things back together as quickly as possible, and to call his insurance company.

"How do we handle this?"

"Leave everytin' to us mister. We are professionals. Foist we board up de window and replace all de broken glass in de rooms. Den we measure up de hallway frame, take samples wid us, and tomorrow we're back wid somethin' yull never tell from noo."

"I don't want 'new'. That frame was over a hundred years old."

"We got older stuff den dat. We grab onto it whenever dey tear down old places like dis."

The men went straight to work boarding up the window, replacing panes, and sweeping up the broken glass. While they were at it Adam went back upstairs and put on a sweat shirt and jeans. He had been straightening up on his own to get started. Any appetite for food had deserted him. It had disintegrated in the wake of this disaster. When he came back downstairs there were three policemen wandering about. The one seeming to be in charge, was immediately off on the wrong foot and reaching for Adam's bad side.

"Mister, I'd say you've got a real security problem here."

"Thanks a lot. Any other suggestions? What do I do? Call in the military?"

"Now don't take it the wrong way. I just mean that if you're not gonna turn on your alarm system, you'd better bar up your first floor windows."

"In case you didn't notice, this is a real fancy neighborhood, not the ghetto."

"Makes no difference. Especially in a wealthy neighborhood, you have to protect yourself. Somebody's probably been casing you."

"So what if the alarm had gone off? You guys took more than a half hour to get here."

"It rattles them or maybe they run for it."

"Or they could get real mad, rip out the alarm, and clobber me?"

"Or worse. It happens."

Adam was at the point of not being sure anymore just whom he resented more, the robbers or the cops. The other two policemen were now busy dusting various things in an apparent effort to recover fingerprints. One of them reported back to the officer in charge.

"Nothin'. Must have worn gloves."

Adam wasn't buying.

"Come on. You telling me you didn't even find my prints on any of those things?"

"Nope."

"Maybe you better go back to school."

The first one chimed in.

"Look mister, we're just doing our job. If he says no prints, the man knows what he's doing. There's no prints. Now why don't we just sit down and you tell me what's missing."

"Why? You know how to get it all back?"

"Maybe. Sometimes we get lucky. And besides which, your insurance company is gonna want a copy of our report."

"That's different."

Adam tried to account for everything that seemed to have been stolen.

"That's all I can think of right now."

"Okay. If you remember anything else, just call it in. But you want a suggestion?"

"I'm all ears."

"Get yourself a dog. Anything that's got a real loud bark. And for me, the meaner the better. If you don't want one that's trained, any male Doberman will fill the bill. They're even smart enough to teach you a thing or two. There's an outfit you can look up called Doberman Rescue. They've got terrific dogs just lookin' for a good home. Won't cost you a dime. You do that, and keep your alarm turned on, and I bet no one'll come anywhere near this place. We gotta go. Three other break-ins to get to."

The cops, and then the repair men, took off. Time finally, with or without appetite, for that ham sandwich.

Nine

That night, after tidying up the place, Adam slept with two loaded shotguns alongside him. One on the floor, the other on top of an adjacent bed. He kept all of his outside lights on and the security system activated. He checked on these precautions a half dozen times or more, as best he could, in his reach for surety. Surety. Always elusive. Always unachievable. And now he feared it would be even harder for him to overcome his relentless checking. If by being as careful about everything as he was, disaster was still this easy to come by, how could he avoid being even more dogged in his compulsive behavior?

Someone else, a reasonable person, by virtue of such a mishap, might take the opposite lead and stop being overly fussy, give up on trying to control everything. Would cast himself upon the waters. Have that kind of a behavioral breakthrough. But not Adam. To the contrary. Odds were, and he knew it, he'd be all the more careful or even try to develop some kind of a program for systematically courting trouble over and over again so as to improve upon his mettle for dealing with it. And unfortunately, he'd experienced a kind of buoyancy, a sort of a lift, from painstakingly putting his furniture back in place and rearranging perfectly the items that had not been stolen.

The next day, when his front doorbell rang, he'd entirely forgotten that Reynolds was due to arrive. Reynolds sensed it as Adam let him in.

"You're not ready? In the middle of something?"

"No, no. It's just that things are a little topsy-turvy around here right now. I had a break-in yesterday afternoon. See where they took out my window?"

"Same thing happened at our house last month. You weren't hurt, were you?"

"Slept right through it. Never knew it was going on."

"Just as well. Whatever they got, nothing is as important as your life. You were lucky."

Adam had quite different ideas.

"Lucky my ass. Now I'm gonna be even more careful. And what's more, all I think about is how the damned guys aren't really gone. It's all still going on. And over and over, I can just about hear them and I get this picture of the bastards fumbling around downstairs. So I grab my gun, head down to where they're at and take them by surprise. There are two of them. I drop the first with a shot in the chest, the second with a round in the head. Then I go back and finish off the first guy in the head also."

"That's crazy."

"Brilliant. How'd you ever come to that conclusion?"

"Why do you have a gun?"

"So I can shoot it. Why else would I have it?"

Reynolds had started to wonder if this was the best time to resume. Maybe, if it was even a good idea to ever do so.

"Want to skip today?"

"No, no. Let's have at it. We can go into the living room."

Once there, Adam settled into an armchair. Reynolds opted for an antique rocker.

"Well. What's going on with the wallet?"

"Not much. At best, if I neither feel for it nor press my butt against it, I'm still thinking about it all the time and trying to reassure myself it's really back there in the pocket where it belongs."

"You shouldn't underestimate what you've accomplished. The main thing is you're not reaching for it. The rest will pass. Particularly as we move on to other matters. And that's precisely what I want you to do right now. Just like we did with the wallet, give us the first thing coming to mind that you'd like to be sure of."

"My gun."

"Your *gun*?"

Reynolds wasn't happy about this. Not happy at all.

"Yeah. The safety. I'm not sure it's on. I know it's on. But naturally, I can't be sure. Should I go and get it? Bring it downstairs?"

"No. Like before with the wallet. Resist. Resist."

"What are you talking about? With the wallet I resisted only after I had it in my pocket. But right now, the safety is where the gun is, upstairs. Seems to me if I'm gonna do this thing right, be consistent about it, I've got to go and get the gun, take the safety off, then slide it back on and try to leave it that way. Not fiddle with it any."

Reynolds clearly did not appreciate this sudden turn.

"What makes you think about the gun, anyway?"

"If it's off when I believe it's on and then I drop it or

bump it, it could misfire and hit something. Like my foot or worse."

Reynolds suddenly went for new methodology, one based upon straightforward argumentation.

"All of this, I'm sure you appreciate, is very unlikely."

Adam was beginning to realize that Reynolds was leery enough about guns to fly in the face of basic behavioral therapy precepts.

"Hey. That's what this is supposed to be all about. Isn't it? The fact that appreciating what's likely or unlikely happens to get me absolutely nowhere. No? Which is what sets off my checking and rechecking. Right?"

"That's one way to look at it."

"Okay then. I'm going for the gun. If you want to chicken out because you're scared or don't hold with people owning guns, just take off. I'll understand. But from all you've been telling me up 'till now, if we're to do this right we've got no options."

Adam headed upstairs noting that Reynolds was holding fast to the arms of the rocker and pressing his knees firmly together. He was still there when he returned but transparently aghast on first sighting Adam as he reentered the room.

"You've got two guns."

"Right. So there wouldn't be any point in just checking one of them, would there?. It looks like they're both okay. See? There's no red dot showing."

Reynolds leaned ever so slightly forward in his rocker as Adam kneeled before him and indicated the position of the safety slide switches for each of his shotguns.

"I see."

"Now I'll move them so you can see the red dot. Okay?"

Reynolds was taking a deep breath.

"I see."

"And now they're both on again. Right?"

"Yes. Yes."

"Now what?"

"Now what? Why, just take them both upstairs and leave them there. And leave the safeties on for God's sake."

"We didn't do it that way with the wallet. We kept it in my pants pocket and I resisted. If we're gonna do it right shouldn't we just lean the shotguns against the wall over there and have me do the same?"

"No, Adam. The wallet was put precisely where it belonged and so should the guns. Which is upstairs, exactly where they were when you first thought about them."

"You're right. I see where you're coming from."

Adam left with the guns but took a full eight minutes to return. By then Reynolds had looked at his watch several times.

"You okay, Adam? You were quite long in coming back."

"I had trouble breaking away. Kept staring at the safeties trying to be sure they were really on. Hope we're not using up valuable time."

"Not at all. You're really catching on to it. That's the important thing. And I assume the guns are out of mind now?"

For Reynolds, the guns being out of sight and out of the room was really what was most essential.

"Hell no. All I'm thinking about is whether or not those red dots are still showing. I better go check it out."

"No. No. Resist, Adam. Resist."

"Shit. This is for the birds. And we haven't even started to deal with the garage doors."

"Now you knew that was to come later."

"How much later?"

"Hard to say."

Adam's exasperation was becoming palpable.

"Try."

"It depends. Depends upon our progress with these other, these lesser compulsions."

"With which I'm doing just brilliantly. Right?"

"I wouldn't exactly put it that way. Rather, it's in keeping with what's to be expected at this stage of the game."

"'Game' is not the right word for it."

"What?"

"You called it a 'game'. Me, I'd call it a scam."

"Adam. Now really."

"Don't get on your high horse with me, buster. The way I see it you're on like a pricey God damned house-to-house road tour in Nutsville. And by the way, what's it gonna come to? I'm willing to bet at least a hundred bucks a stopover."

"Seventy-five."

"Still no bargain. No bargain because I don't figure you as much of a helpmate for this particular customer since we are getting nowhere and we're doin' it slowly. I'm suspicious about the whole deal. How many customers you see in one day?"

"I have evening hours also. Some of my patients can't leave work. All told, about eight or nine each twenty four hours."

"So when do you have an opening for somebody new? After a suicide?"

"There's only been one suicide that I know of."

"Is that how I got my slot?"

"No, Adam. Some patients drop out. Get to where they can manage on their own."

"Manage?"

"Of course. With medication and a first hand knowledge of the principles of this sort of thing, patients usually learn to cope. Mine is just a helping hand needed at the outset."

"The way I see it your hand is only helping itself to seventy five bucks a throw from anyone you can manage to line up. And if your kind of 'coping' is at best something like that sixty odd percent improvement figure Rogoff swears is all that's out there, no matter which way I go, medication, psychotherapy, your kinda trip, or the whole kit-n-caboodle, then brother, I want no part of it. Because it's clear to me that if ever we do get past the wallet business and the gun deal, and make it out to the fucking garage, which I'm beginning to seriously doubt, then maybe, just maybe, I'll tear myself away from checking the damned garage doors in thirty seconds instead of the minute and a half I've been used to putting in at it. Big deal. Big fucking deal!"

Reynolds had been shaking his head in ardent disagreement through all of this.

"That's not the way to look at it. There's the matter, the important matter of feeling better, of just getting to feel better. And I promise you that you will feel better, less depressed for each and every time you make it even a little easier on yourself."

"Yeah? Lay that one on the Horla."

"The what?"

"Forget it. And let's just forget this whole screwy deal. I'm passing. I'm passing on all of it."

"I don't understand."

"There's gotta be a better way. But if this is all there is, it's not for me. Look Reynolds, thanks for nothing. Now I'm gonna see you out but don't forget. Send me the bill."

Reynolds was determined to hang on to the end.

"Should you change your mind..."

"Yeah, yeah. I'll buzz you. And again, you forgot my bagels."

So what? So he'd just stay sequestered in his house and tough this thing through. Whatever he'd need, he'd order up by telephone. What was there to go outside for, anyway? He couldn't work any more and as for Rogoff, why not see if he might allow him telephone hours? He'd read somewhere that such arrangements were feasible. Psychiatrists even practiced that way long distance for patients who had moved away. And in a couple of days he'd up the dose of Prozac once more. Maybe he'd get some kind of a boost out of it. But so far, any effect was equivocal.

He was torn from these considerations by the doorbell. The window repair guys were back with what looked like a perfect replica of his front hall window.

The foreman was justly proud of their work.

"What did we tell yuh? Can't tell it from de original, right?"

"No doubt about it. It's a terrific job."

In less than an hour the men had removed the temporary plywood panels, secured the replacement window to the frame, and were gone.

What next? Like the cop had suggested, a dog. He'd try to arrange for a nice and nasty Doberman. But as Adam reached for his Yellow Pages the phone rang. It was Miranda.

"Hey, how are you? You know something? You can really worry a person."

"Well right now, everything is under control. But I've gotta tell you, yesterday afternoon they broke in here while I was taking a nap and..."

"Who?"

"How the hell would I know? For sure it's nobody I hang out with."

"Sorry."

"That's okay... I really appreciate your calling me. And I just fired the behavioral guy. We were getting nowhere and doing it too slowly. Which leaves me with nothing much to do right now except to bring in a real tough guard dog. One of the cops thought it was a good idea. You want to stop by?"

"Oh God" was all Miranda could say.

"He isn't over there, is he? Listen. I'm open to any neat ideas, from whomever. There's not a prejudiced bone in my body, except for the bastards who busted in here."

"With you it gets worse and worse, doesn't it?"

"Yeah. That's how he works it."

"Who's he?"

"Hey you forgetting? The Horla. That's who he is. My unwanted buddy."

"Oh God."

"You've already said that. So you comin' over? How about bringin' a pizza? But not just any old pizza, a serious pizza like in the old country. There's a place called Valentino's just opened up on Wisconsin Avenue where they do the baking in a special high temp brick oven and..."

"Stop it, Adam. Stop it. Stop it."

"Hey? This really Miranda?"

"Of course it is."

"The one who wants to know how I'm doin'?"

"I take it back, Adam. Look. I'm still at work and real busy. Call you later."

Well that was nice. Really nice. Great to know somebody out there was thinking of him. Who'd figure it'd be a gal he'd only met the other night and seemed not too sad to send him on his way? His mood was somewhat bolstered by Miranda's solicitous inclinations. He reached for the phone book again and located the appropriate number. A man responded.

"Hello?"

"This Doberman to the rescue?"

"You some kind of a joker? It's Harry Goldberg for Doberman Rescue Society. How can we help you?"

"I need a dog. Something real vicious."

"Look mister, we don't have any vicious dogs. Just well-bred Dobermans that need a good home. And we don't place any of them without checking out the people real careful like. Why do you want this kinda dog, anyway?"

"I had a break in and the cops suggested it. But I love dogs, always used to have one when the kids were growing up and right now I'm alone and could appreciate the company."

Except for the bit about the cops and the break in it was all lies, lies, lies. Adam had no children, nor had he ever owned a dog. But he could pretty well guess at what it was going to take for him to come by one of these specialized brutes from Doberman Rescue.

Goldberg seemed more receptive.

"You looking for a male or a female?"

Adam guessed a male would be the more aggressive but didn't dare to give that reason for his choice.

"I think a retired widower like me should go for a male."

"Okay... A black dog or a red one?"

"Like I was just telling someone else, I have absolutely no prejudices."

"Come on, mister. Get serious."

"I'll go for black."

Adam could just about see this monster, in the dark of night, his eyes glowering, lip curled, a low pitched reverberating rumble emanating from his chest, backside hair raised and bristling, and at his loyal ready near the foot of his master's bed prepared to hurl himself down the stairs on the barest provocation and grab any God damned intruder by the throat.

"Okay... Right now there's a two year old black male set for placement. I'd need to go and check him out. Haven't seen him in a month but he's neutered and a very nice dog. The couple that's got him both work and their kid's in school all day long so the dog's had to stay in the basement 'till they all get home. They've come to realize that their setup isn't right for the dog and are ready to give him up. He's even had obedience training and is housebroken. The way I see it, it's a real good deal."

"What do I have to do?"

"Nothing. Just give me your address. At five o'clock I'll head on out there and pick up the dog and if he's okay I'll bring him over to your place. Depending on how he reacts, and how you check out, we can choose or not choose to leave him. That's it. You gonna be home?"

"Absolutely. Christ. I hope you guys give me the green light."

"See you later then."

Given his big house and roomy fenced in backyard, Adam took Doberman Rescue approval for granted and ordered two dog mats, lamb and rice dog food, as well as a couple of leather dog chews from the local pet shop. All of this was delivered in a half hour and soon Adam had placed one mat at the foot of his bed and the other in the front hall beneath the window that had been so rudely violated. He inspected the backyard to be sure there were no breaks in the chain link fence or other places a dog might easily dig out.

While in the yard the thought did cross his mind that perhaps two dogs might be an even better idea with one of them serving as a backup or if need be sheltered outside in a dog house, at the ready to intercept intruders before they could even get any fancy ideas. But he'd keep that possibility on a back burner for now until he saw how this first animal worked out.

Ten

A t six-thirty the front door bell sounded persistently. Adam barely saw the man standing there because as soon as the door went wide he went reeling backwards. A very large and true to description black Doberman had reared up and driven both of his front paws deeply into Adam's chest. Goldberg, a smallish and stocky fellow with gray hair and motley beard, holding as fast as he might to a very taut dog lead, was unaccountably pleased by this bit of canine shenanigan.

"He likes you. That's a solid sign of it."

"I thought you said he was obedience trained."

Goldberg didn't answer, just closed the door securely behind him and briefly looked about as the dog proceeded to smell Adam's shoes.

"Okay... Let's see what he does when I turn him loose."

In an instant the dog was everywhere with the two of them in hardly competent pursuit. Nose to the floor, he bounded from room to room, kitchen, dining room, living room, den, front hall, up and down the stairs, into each bed room, over and around the beds, investigating every nook and cranny, sniffing at anything in his path. Finally, Adam and Goldberg, the two of them substantially out of breath, sat down in the den content to just bear stationary witness to the dog's perpetual motion. Goldberg was reassuring.

"Once he's smelled everything in sight he'll settle down. Meanwhile let's see what's outside."

Adam showed him the backyard facilities and when they were inside again, the dog mats and other provisions. Goldberg looked quite pleased. By then the dog was resting on the mat in the front hall and working very diligently at a leather chew. As they returned to the den the dog stuck steadfastly to his mat. Goldberg came right to the point.

"Okay... He's yours or you're his and I'll be on my way. This paper explains everything you need to know about his shots and stuff. His name is Willy."

"Willy?"

"What's wrong with that?"

"Nothing. But it's not considered bad luck, is it? If I should give him a new name? Like with a boat?"

"Not that I've heard of. Call him what you want. You two are on your own."

When Goldberg exited Willy never rose from his mat. He just kept working on his chew which Adam noted was very rapidly going to shreds and pieces. Terrific teeth and jaws. And exactly what the job description called for. With the front door closed behind him, Adam knelt down and spoke to his dog.

"Hey there doggy. How you doin'?"

His first and very own dog responded with a growl. There was also that deep throated rumble and curled lip he'd only imagined a little while before. The problem was, they were now directed at him, the ostensible master.

Also, the dog, shortly back to gnawing what was left of his leather chew had him blocked against the entrance doorway. Without an assured safe passage by him, he couldn't chance to change his position and so was forced to stay where he was crouched down in front of the dog and eyeing rather apprehensively Willy's all too efficient demolishment of the rawhide.

After awhile he caught on to what was happening. The dog was merely guarding his chew. Fortunately, there was another one and it lay right there on a table beside him, in an unopened package. As soon as Adam reached for it, the dog was up, allowed the spent chew to drop from his mouth and was wagging his stump of Doberman tail appreciatively. Adam offered Willy the brand new delicacy and as he did so, stepped quickly by him.

Now Willy seemed to comprehend what Adam represented by way of dog to man bonding. Adam constituted an apparently unlimited supply of things this dog had previously, probably, only dreamed of. And thus the bonding process began. Wherever Adam went, with chew in mouth the dog would follow. They were glued. Even when Adam went to the john, the dog was right there beside him. In fact, in the interest of privacy, if he so much as dared to shut him out by closing the door against him, Willy would bark with such God awful stridency, Adam had no option but to yield and give him entry. Then, while Adam tended to his toilet or at least attempted to do so, the dog, appreciatively, would lick his face.

Later on, Adam called Goldberg to inquire why this Willy animal refused to tolerate exclusion from him.

"When you do that to him the dog gets what we call 'separation anxiety'. I forgot to tell you about it."

"Meaning?"

"It's no big deal. He won't actually bite you if you insist on leaving him. He'll just jump up and down and bark his fool head off. You see, when the couple who raised him left him in their basement all day long, the poor guy hated it. So he got in the habit of raising all hell every damned time they tried to put him down there. I'm afraid there's not much you can do about it. But if you're interested in having protection, you couldn't do better. That dog will never leave your side. Just don't let him get up in the bed with you. That could be a nuisance. Kick him out if you have to. Make him use the dog mat on the floor."

"Make him?"

"Sure. Draw the line. You have to come down real hard on Dobermans or they'll take you over. Especially a male. They can be one tough customer."

"He won't turn on me, will he?"

"Hey. This is a dog, not a wild animal. If he senses that you actually intend to hurt him he's gonna get down to business and do what he does best. But he's smart enough to know it when all you're trying to do is teach him what you want or don't want him to do. Don't fret it. That there dog's gonna read you like a book. He's got senses you never even dreamed of. Take care now."

Adam turned to his new companion.

"That right Willy?"

No comment from Willy.

"Listen up guy. You partial to that handle of yours?"

Again no comment. Just uninterrupted mastication and overly attentive staring.

"Because for me 'Willy' is like willy-nilly and not exactly what I have in mind as your up-and-coming life role around here. If it's okay with you, from now on you're my dog 'Savage'. How's that grab you?"

The dog, quite obviously, could either take it or leave it.

"Then 'Savage' it is."

To celebrate this momentous event, Adam decided to give Savage a first meal in his new home. It consisted of sixteen carefully measured ounces of a premium lamb and rice mix spilled into a brand new porcelain doggy feeding bowl. For the sake of accuracy he utilized one of his former wife's favorite measuring cups. Savage dropped his leather chew, ambled over to sniff at the dog food, and then walked uninterestedly away to resume his jawing of the chew.

"Hey man. Goldberg said you haven't had anything to eat today. What's up?"

Adam had raised his voice a bit more than was required for mere appropriate protestation of unsatisfactory canine feeding behavior and once more Savage began to rumble.

"Okay, okay, you're right. You're right. When you're right, you're right. Let's see if there's something we can spice it up with, make it more interesting."

There was some leftover chicken breast in the fridge. Adam tore it into pieces and placed them on top of the dog food. Now Savage dashed to the bowl gulped down the chicken, but only the chicken, and returned to his chew.

"Come on, man."

Again that threatening growl.

"Okay, okay. Whatever you say."

The dog had the appearance of being well fed, so what urgency could there be, anyway, for pushing him to eat? Also, Adam recalled having read somewhere that guard dogs shouldn't be fed too much, especially late in the day. So best to cool it, let the poor guy get adjusted and sooner of later his appetite would probably catch up with him. Adam settled for attaching Savage's leash and putting him through his paces in the backyard in line with instructions he'd gotten from Goldberg. The dog was observed to walk nicely on his left side to heel, to sit, and even to stay when commanded to do so. Adam was beginning to feel extremely impressed both with this dog and the whole idea of having him.

At nine o'clock Adam was back in the kitchen, half way through another sandwich. It was of chicken he'd managed to hold back for himself. Savage was alongside the table and nudging him, intently eyeing each mouthful, and transparently hopeful of snatching more of the same for himself. When the wall phone rang, Adam quickly grabbed for it but at the same time he strategically lifted what remained of his minimal meal to a high counter top, presumably beyond the reach of his dog.

"You been out?"

It was Miranda again.

"No. Well maybe for a few minutes when I was in the backyard with Savage."

"Who?"

"My new dog. His name is Savage. It used to be Willy but I renamed him."

"Where'd you say that pizza place was?"

"Yeah? Terrific. Corner of Wisconsin and Calvert. Like I said, it's called Valentino's. I'd send out for it but they do it real authentic and are tryin' to be up market so they won't deliver. Make mine with anchovies. You know where I live, right?"

"You feeling any better, Adam?"

"Well I'm a hell of lot more secure than I was this afternoon."

"Why's that?"

"You'll see when you get here."

"Look Adam. That dog isn't gonna go for me, is he?"

"No more than me, kid. Don't worry. He's completely under my control."

"All right. I'm on my way".

There was no need to save what was left of his sandwich. Savage had been able to negotiate the countertop and had wolfed it down while Adam was on the phone.

"How the hell did you get all the way up there?"

Again he'd not hit on the right degree of vigor in calling to account such a high-strung fellow and Savage responded accordingly.

"Never you mind. I'll try to be more careful. And it was rotten of me to tempt you like that."

To get ready for Miranda he changed into fresh jeans and shirt and then set the dining room table for two. It was a handsome room, darkly oak paneled with a large fireplace. Before the split with his wife he'd spent many fall and winter evenings there, pleased to eat fine food before an open fire. But that was then and this was now. It was springtime and there'd be no fire, his mind was presumably set to self destruct, and only a mere pizza would be placed before him, this demanding dog, and a woman who was practically a stranger.

Although he wouldn't drink because of the Prozac, he opened a fine bottle of wine and centered it on the table. It was an eighty-eight Brown Brother's Cabernet from Australia, a great vineyard and a good year. The simple presence of the wine seemed to engender a bit of the room's old enchantment. Without doubt, lovely Miranda's incursion would contribute even more.

Peculiar, her decision first to call and now to come over. His home, after all, under its present circumstances, which were well conveyed to her, could hardly sound like a settled place to be. And she had looked, if anything, in no small a hurry to split from him the other night. So what gave here? Was there going to be a coming together?

For quite some time thoughts like that had managed to be no more than dissociated speculations. That is, dissociated from either emotion or physical arousal. Rogoff said the onus for all of this could be laid to depression, depression over his obsessive-compulsiveness. It might just be. But right now he felt keyed up and it sure had nothing to do with his having fired Reynolds or what might be rubbing off on him from this dedicated dog.

When Miranda rang the bell Adam confined Savage to the den, whereupon the dog began to throw himself at the intervening door and to bark furiously. There was no alternative to this exclusion because Adam could not afford to have the dog run by him and right on out into the street. If that happened Savage might take off and disappear. Or worse, lunge at Miranda and knock her down. She entered into what must have seemed bedlam's special province.

"What the hell is going on? Sounds like a damned kennel."

Adam closed the front door quickly and had her sit in a chair.

"No. It's only a single dog but he's got this attitude about being left out of things. It's called separation anxiety."

"It figures. Now you've begun to drive animals batty."

"Just stay sitting there so you don't seem threatening to him and I'll let him in. Once he smells you and sees you're one of the good guys there'll be no problem. I'll just hide the pizza as a precaution. He seems to only like people food."

"Suppose he doesn't go for my smell?"

"Impossible. Okay... Here he comes."

Adam gave Savage his release.

"Get this hound off of me!"

Savage had barely taken a single whiff of her before he'd placed both front paws astride Miranda's thighs and launched a lickfest upon her face. There seemed to be no denying him and not only was he bussing her adamantly, but before Adam realized what he was up to he had enfolded her left leg between both of his two rear ones and had begun to rock his pelvis back and forth to a rhythm of provocative implications.

"Off. Savage. Off."

"Come on, Adam. This damned dog is trying to rape me!"

Adam had no recourse but to attach Savage's lead and to pull him away from Miranda and out of the front hall. Then the dog settled down graciously, wagged his abbreviated tail, and was soon content to simply follow them into the dining room.

"Sorry about that. But you've got to give the guy credit. He's got excellent taste."

"You give him credit. I'd like to swat him."

"If I were you I wouldn't even think about doing something like that. Love at first sight could easily turn into love spurned and then there'd be all hell to pay."

"Just keep him off of me. And let's eat before the pizza's cold. Eating, if you remember is my real passion. Oh my, isn't this a lovely room! And you've got a wine bottle all opened up and breathing nice and easy. Splendid."

"Here. Let me put half in the oven. I've got it all warmed up."

"Do I have to pour my own wine?"

"Sorry about that. There you go. I'll be right back."

When he returned it was to find her in high spirits, savoring the wine and chomping pizza down at incredible speed. Savage was sitting beside her, staring up at her face attentively.

"Why's this dog staring at me?"

"It's not for love alone anymore. Now it's for pizza alone. Be sure and keep your plate on the other side of the table or every last bit of it'll be gone in a flash. So then, to what do Savage and I owe our good fortune?"

"Isn't this crust unusual? It's so light and so crisp. And the tomato and everything tastes so fresh."

Adam bit into his own slice.

"Like I told you. You can't find anything like this anywhere else in town. Eat one of these and other pizzas are the pits. You gonna answer the question?"

"I found I was worrying about you. Providence must have decided I should lend a hand. And I'm not used to meeting someone this way. So it's probably for a reason."

"You're sounding a little mystical."

"Maybe it's my father talking. He was Irish."

"Okay... That explains it."

"Look. Let's just cease with all of this drivel. I'm going to eat while the food's still hot, or at least warm, and if you've still got any sense at all, you'll do the same. The wine, by the way is superb, absolutely divine. And later on, unless you can think of something better, we'll go to bed, that's together I mean. Because crazy as you may be, I've decided I go for you. I'll even stay the night. That's unless this monster dog of your has other ideas."

Adam was flabbergasted.

"You go for me?"

"Adam. Don't bother me until I finish this slice."

She ate relentlessly then recommenced. "All right. So before you go to the oven for the rest of my supper I should draw you some kind of a diagram? Correct? 'Going for you' means I've decided that this relationship of ours, from my standpoint, is cleared for being open-ended. I should confess to having the hots for you? Forget it. I should talk about love or chemistry? Not on your life. In a little while I'll be ready to go to bed. That's it. Now go get the rest of my pizza so I can finish up. You do the same, and I suppose you'll have to let the dog out for whatever. Then we'll see what really cooks. How about it?"

"You make it sound so easy."

Adam hastened to do as instructed with minor variance. After serving Miranda the remaining warmed half of her pizza and pouring her another glass of Cabernet, he wrapped his own pie in aluminum foil and stored it in the refrigerator. Then, calling to Savage, he led the dog outside to the backyard, staying there until he did what had to be done. Things were proceeding like clockwork. It seemed that both the animal and he were now obliged to do, promptly and exactly, as she'd commanded.

When he returned to the dining room Miranda had finished eating. Wine in hand she was admiring a tapestry attached to one of the walls.

"That must have cost a fortune."

"Six hundred bucks."

"You're kidding."

"Nope. It's only an Aubusson copy. But I did manage to bargain it down from two grand."

"How?"

"The way I usually do. I make my bid and if they say no deal, I walk out of the place. Every once in awhile, if the guy's hungry enough, he comes running after me. That time, I was nearly a block away."

"Neat."

"Yeah, I kinda think so. Notice it's done up in wool? Most copies are cotton or even synthetic... So the dog's been out and I put the rest of my pizza in the refrigerator."

"Anything else you have to do while I finish my wine?"

"The usual. That's all."

"Which is?"

"Lock up the place, turn on the alarm and ... check a few things."

"Okay... You do that. I'll just take the wine upstairs and get comfortable."

"Hey. I'd probably get it done faster if you came along."

"You want to ruin everything? You want to take a chance like that?"

"Come on Miranda. You did it for me in the bar and at the Kennedy Center. Give me a break and help out."

"All right. Lay on MacDuff. No pun intended."

Adam led Miranda, wine glass in hand, to the back door, located behind the kitchen.

"See? I take a good look at the lock making sure the dead bolt slider is in place. I even press up on it to be certain it's really in the right position. Ordinarily, I do that several times."

"Not tonight you don't. We are short on time."

"That's what I'm hoping for. You know, my behavioral therapist guy never even came back here with me."

"What are you doing now?"

"Just pressing against the slider some. Making sure."

"Enough. The door is locked. And stop pulling on the handle like that. You'll sunder it."

"Okay. I think I'm set to go over there and turn on the alarm."

"So do it."

Adam walked across the kitchen to a security panel on the wall and proceeded to tap in his code numbers whereupon there was a female voice announcing that the system was set for 'LEVEL TWO'. That fact could also be read from a monitor screen which was part of the unit.

"We're done now?"

"It says 'LEVEL TWO'?"

"Absolutely."

"You're sure?"

"I never lie."

"I'll take just one more look at it."

"You do and I'm out of here."

The threat had instantaneous effect. He moved away from the panel and through a hallway leading back into the dining room. Was his libido finally coming to the fore and measuring up to what he'd theorized was necessary for serious confrontation with the Horla?

"Terrific. You're helping a lot. I'd a been back there much longer without you doing all of this. It's like I got not only support but incentive to break away."

"Can we go upstairs now?"

"Only thing left is to turn off the inside lights... There. That does it. And check that the outside ones are on."

"You don't have to do that. They were on when I came in."

"You sure?"

"Adam. Guess what happens if you ask me that just one more time."

"Gotcha."

"I should hope so. At least sooner or later."

He led the way upstairs and into the main bedroom. Savage, already familiar with his own designated spot, had settled down on his mat at the foot of the bed. Miranda questioned the wisdom of this setup.

"That where he's gonna be?"

"Sweetheart, this is a first night for him also and to tell the truth, I'm not positive what he'd do if I started to shut the bedroom door on him. But I can tell you this. Even when I began to close him out of the john he barked and howled bloody murder and was ready to tear the place apart."

"Look, Adam. That fool dog has already tried to hump me. And with absolutely no provocation. What happens when we start breathing heavy and tossin' around?"

"Don't ask me. Your guess is as good as mine."

"Great. Just great. Obsessive-compulsive foolishness laced maybe with some kind of doggy voyeurism or even worse. Where do I hang my clothes? You got a bathroom in this nuthouse of yours?"

"Sure. But wouldn't it be nicer if first we sort of kissed a little?"

"Oh God. A sentimental clown to boot. Come here and we'll start it off your way."

It had been a put-on. She'd been joking her way through all of this only to temper a turbulence. Adam knew it as soon as he offered her a gentle kind of kiss. More of a caress, actually, than a kiss. Because her response was hardly the same. All at once she was so passionate he had to break for air.

"You need the bathroom, do you?"

"Not at all! But you go and if Savage trots along with you that's all right with me. I'll just toss my clothes on that chair and hop into bed."

In barely a minute he was there beside her hardly caring any further about where Savage might or might not be. And needing no more preliminaries than it seemed she did, they were instantly as one. There was no alternative. And how incredible it was, at least for those precious few moments, to be free, entirely free. In fact the damned house, like in the story, could just about burn down around them. Burglars could be sneaking up the stairs. Even the Horla could be right there, leering, gnashing his teeth. Nothing mattered except to feel her mouth and tongue upon his, her thighs clasped around his thighs, to smell her fragrance and to keep pressing down in a steady rhythm as she gasped and moaned with satisfaction until finally she had something to communicate.

"Okay, okay, you're about to kill me."

"But I haven't finished yet."

"Why not? You were sure big as hell. Christ, you're still big as hell."

"I dunno. Up until now I've only had the opposite kind of problem. Not all the time, but on occasion."

"Now you tell me."

"This is real frustrating."

It sure was. Adam was dying, just dying to let go inside this wondrous gal.

"Here, let me try and help you."

Miranda wriggled out from under him and tried another, not exactly biblical, but still a commonly reliable and age old approach. After awhile she saw, and he accepted, that they were getting nowhere. It was time to reach some kind of a conclusion, not only physical but also diagnostic.

"I'd say you've got a problem."

"No kidding."

"Well there's nothing we can do but sleep on it."

And that's what she rolled over and managed to do. Savage, who oddly enough hadn't even stirred from his mat during any of their gymnastics, began to snore. Adam, in a state of slow decompression and feeling lower than ever, wondered if the Horla, after all, had had still another and even more sinister way with him.

Sleep, that night, was more difficult than ever to come by. And now the tempting fragrance of the beautiful woman beside him was a cruel twist indeed.

Eleven

In the morning, Miranda was up and ready to leave with barely time to shower. Adam, perplexed as ever and reduced to feeling beached and useless, was eagerly solicitous.

"Come on. At least have some coffee or maybe a glass of orange juice."

"Hey. Don't make like a Jewish mother! You like orange juice? Drink orange juice."

"You're disappointed in me?"

"Hell no. Disappointed with a guy who won't stop until I beg for mercy? You kidding? I know gals who'd kill for someone like that. Don't you worry about me. You just get yourself checked out and understand that I feel, I really do feel for your little problem."

"Little?"

"Adam. I'm sure you realize that dwelling on something like this is only gonna make it worse. Go talk to a... what do you call them? I forget."

"Urologist."

"Right. A urologist. Good heavens, I'm late already.

Hold onto that damned dog and turn off the alarm before I set it off. I'm out of here!"

"Call me."

Before settling for a urological examination Adam was soon considering one other possibility. He had to reread the manufacturer's drug warning for Prozac handed him by the pharmacist. While Miranda had been asleep he'd hit upon the possibility that the medication might be the culprit. It took a good bit of searching but finally he found it lodged in the inside pocket of the jacket he'd worn to Rogoff's office. It said nothing about this kind of problem.

He decided, however, to touch one other base with the same question. He'd quiz Rogoff. Because it was still too early for Rogoff to be in his office and knowing how much the man hated to be bothered at home, he showered, had breakfast of juice, ham, eggs, and coffee, and wondered about this 'Jewish mother' label being pinned on him. At nine o'clock sharp, he called his doctor, who picked up immediately.

"Hello?"

"Secretary's not in yet?"

"Never is at this hour. It's Adam, right? Who'd have guessed?"

"Come on man. Try and be nice. I'm in even more trouble. Maybe big trouble."

"With Reynolds? You did something stupid?"

"No, no, that's not it at all. Him, I simply canned. That stuff he's into is one big joke."

"Oh God. God help me. Help us all. Please God. Even if it's this early in the morning."

"Are you still at it? What's with this religious thing? It's really getting out of hand."

"Come on, Adam. I have a patient in ten minutes. What's up?"

"I'm not a patient? What am I, chopped liver? I beg to differ. And for your information, what's up is not the problem. Getting it up is now a breeze. Getting it down, in the usual way, the way that satisfies, that's another thing entirely."

"You've got priapism?"

"What's that?"

Quickly, Rogoff defined it for him.

"No. I don't have any damned priapism. What I have is a terrific woman and I'm not able to go. If I try any harder I'll drop dead in the saddle just like old Rockefeller. What I wanta know is does this have anything to do with the Prozac? What the druggist gave me to read says nothing about something like that."

"It's the Prozac."

"Just that simple? How come?"

"It's been reported to cause sexual dysfunction. What the pharmacist gave you to read isn't the whole story. But it is described in the official drug insert. Maybe not entirely clearly. But it's sure there."

"How come you didn't warn me?"

"Well... most people when they're depressed, which is the main indication for prescribing Prozac, don't give a rap about sex just as long as they get to feeling better. And it's not until recently that we've started to appreciate the problem is more common than the drug company was letting on. They admitted to around four percent. Now we know it's more like twenty, maybe even higher."

"So you've ruined me. Right?"

"Don't be ridiculous Adam. It's not permanent. Once

you stop the drug you'll be right back to normal in a matter of days. And there are other serotonin uptake inhibitors
with shorter half lives that we can switch you over to.
Then you can take what's known as a drug holiday, let's
say on a weekend, and do all right by yourself."

"Hey. I don't do it by myself. And I can't exactly
schedule my personal life, even such as it is, with all that
fucking precision. If you get what I mean. Man. I can't
believe this. You a doctor, and me needing to explain it
to you that these things generally happen only when the
spirit moves us."

"Well there's another drug in the same class without
sexual side effects but it isn't too good for obsessive-
compulsive disorder."

"So what's the point?"

"There isn't any. I was just thinking out loud."

It was more than a little too much.

"Thinking? You call what you've been doing, thinking? First you tell me I'm not gonna feel anything at all
for two weeks on this stuff. I take one dose, the world
is gorgeous, and I'm floating like on cloud nine. Second
dose and I'm out in left field. Couldn't even tell what
day it was. And no time is there any real promise from
you that this wonder drug is gonna make me well. I've
just about had to wring it from you that there's a limited
chance of only an uncertain amount of improvement. And
now that I've had the whammy that is the mother of all
whammies, you confess to me that in exchange for all of
this absolute bullshit I'm slated to give up my manhood.
Doc. You are something else. Got any other surprises up
your pharmacological sleeve? Any other booby traps set
and waitin' for me?"

"Adam. All this over one foiled ejaculation?"

"Man. Guys your age shouldn't practice on us young bucks. You just can't relate. One foiled ejaculation? That's what you call it? Christ. It would have been the lay of a lifetime. It was gonna be metaphysical."

Rogoff couldn't spare any more time for either explanations or pleadings that Adam get reasonable.

"Adam, I try to do my best. I always give it my best. That's all I can do. But right now I simply must break away."

"Break a leg."

"What?"

"That's show biz talk for good luck to you. But in this case you can take it literally."

Adam set the phone aside. What a conundrum. And what conceivable way was there to maybe outfox the resurrected Horla? There would certainly be no benefit from taking further Prozac which he would have no more of. Nor from seeing Reynolds. He and his kind were probably just a bunch of money grubbers, working a shrewd gimmick. And as for Rogoff? If Adam's condition represented some kind of a biological fault or bad circuit needing to be mended, Rogoff had shown no particular aptitude for sorting it out. Maybe he, now a victim to early dotage, had become cold, even indifferent, and no more than a fund of misinformation, or a kind of psychological traffic cop pointing the way to Nowheresville. Rogoff was surely no creative bearer of useful or individually tailored clinical revelations.

So what was left? Settle for what he had become? Make peace with his Horla and simply yield to the incessant demands of his infernally flawed brain, ganged up on at this time in his life by some kind of a deviant genetic programmer bent on arranging for a run amuck behavioral future? Become a dedicated checker of almost everything? Cower in the prison of the only mind he'd been dealt and would ever possess from here on in, albeit a rotting one? And all the while be hankering for what he had once been, a quick and ready political wheeler-dealer? And accept a life of mortal envy for guys like Maestro Maazel racing through time in a whirlwind of glory with not a moment to second think, much less check out anything? No way. There wasn't even the ghost of a chance he'd knuckle down to a deal like that.

"Right, Savage?"

He nudged his dog, resting on the floor beside him, gently he thought, with the toe of one loafer. Savage growled fiercely and went for it. Adam was lucky to only have it wrested from his foot. Had the dog had his way the foot itself would probably have been torn off. As it was, Savage now quite proud of himself, headed upstairs with the loafer in his mouth.

"Come back here."

Adam followed him to the second floor and grabbed for his shoe. Then began a man versus dog tug-of-war, Adam pulling and entreating as the dog growled and knuckled down, prepared to hold fast by digging deeply into one of Adam's best oriental carpets. Adam learned very fast that such contests are always won by the dog, unless the animal can be lured away by something provocative. So, as he'd done on the previous day, he offered Savage a more interesting chew, this time a biscuit he had in his pocket. Savage dropped the shoe. Only a short time before, it had been relatively new. It was not, any longer. Far from it. Savage had terrifically sharp teeth. If only somehow he could nail the Horla in much the same way.

Also, this rowdy dog had abundant determined pugnacity and Adam sensed a kind of foreshadowing, perhaps, of eventual like mindedness in himself. Might they not hole up and stay holed up together, these two, making do? Theirs could be a common stand, taking on a common fate, with Savage setting the tone for all of it.

As for checking and double checking, how much of that could there be if all Savage and he needed was to go back and forth to the backyard? And screw the garage doors. Hell. If he never raised them they'd not need to be checked. They'd sure stay right where they were, frozen in place, fixed, down. As for his two cars, they could just about rust where they stood for all he cared. After all, he wasn't going anywhere and had no need of them. It was settled.

Well then. One further thought.

Since he had no need for continued concern regarding interference by booze with the purported therapeutic effects of Prozac, and since this was a just about inspirational moment, why not commemorate it by having himself a little drink even if it was scarcely midday? Why not indeed. Well, because Goldberg, at the time of his interview, had queried him closely about household consumption of alcohol, Doberman Rescue being under rigid mandate to not leave dogs with drunks. Although at that time he was honestly sworn in this dicey matter, by all fair reconsideration, he could really see no reason now for Savage not to make up his own mind in the matter. Last he knew it was a free country for everyone, Dobermans included.

It would be a jigger, just one little jigger of Cardhu, his currently favored single malt. The kind of drink he'd interrupted, actually, on the occasion of running into his lovely new swain at the Mayflower hotel. Savage agreed to it wholeheartedly, provided he got another biscuit.

Back downstairs, then, for the two of them, Adam and his lively dog. He got what was needed from the liquor cabinet and the pantry and was soon in the living room sipping at his scotch. Meanwhile, Savage finished his second biscuit and now alternated between sprawling before him, as part of the dedicated process of bonding, and dashing about the place from room to room, window to window, door to door, erupting loudly at every outside sound or transient glimpse of cats, squirrels, birds. Even when he spotted through the window a tiny butterfly fluttering near the fence a good twenty feet away, the dog went bonkers.

Soon, Adam was feeling quite comfortable. It wasn't at all hard to take, this sitting there in his soft leather armchair and having nothing to do save for watching Savage being Savage, that is, doing whatever he thought the situation called for.

Thought? The dog thought? Savage couldn't possibly do that. Also, he couldn't possibly ever get into Adam's fix and say to himself, "Hey you really lock that door? You really turn off that faucet? Hey you leave the stove on? Forget to plug the toaster out? Hey. Hey. Hey. Hey."

And "situation?" What "situation?" What in all hell did this dog consider the unquestionable sine qua non for a real heavy down home kind of a bark, or a growl, for that matter? Who could ever come up with an answer to such a question? Who would presume to fathom the mind of a dog? "Mind"? That was another one. This dog, of course, didn't have what you could rightly call a mind. And that's why this dog was one hell of a lucky person, this dog was, this here dog. And that's why the next drink was going to be to him. In his bloody honor. And it was time now to go and get it. Which he did, Savage trailing alongside him.

Settling down again in the same chair, Adam thought it a reasonably good idea to turn on his audio system and hear once again the other night's Mahler Ninth, but this one was performed not by Maazel or Von Karajan but by Leonard Bernstein with the Vienna. So he listened but continued to marvel over his steadfast canine companion who now manifested the uncanny ability, irrespective of the fury or the loud volume of a particular musical passage, to still pick up on outside noises apparently beyond human hearing, or at least beyond Adam's kind of human hearing, and to resume his protest of them in a stridently violent, but for Adam, an engagingly more and more endearing manner. Adam was all out taken with his dog.

When the phone rang in the adjoining room he decided to ignore it. The next time, however, it rang long enough for the answering machine to pick up and to convey the sound of Miranda's voice starting to leave a message. He ran for the other room and picked up.

"Don't hang up. We're here."

"What are you two up to?"

"I'm listening to the Ninth. I can't tell what he's hearing, but he's been barking his head off all morning."

"What else is new?"

"The deal is it was the Prozac. I got Rogoff to make a full confession."

"And?"

"So I stopped taking it."

"That's awful."

"How you figure that? You mean for you? Think I'm only hot stuff if I'm on a damned drug? You could at least wait to see how I do once I'm off it."

"That's not what I mean, silly. I mean how are you going to get well, now? If you're off the drug and you've given up on Reynolds too, what else is there? What will you do?"

"Lay around. My dog and me are set to lay around and tough it out. Maybe he'll come up with something."

"You been drinking?"

"How'd you tell? Him and me were kinda celebrating until you rang us up."

"I can smell it all the way over here."

"Where's that?"

"My place. I came home for lunch and to pick up some papers I need. Want to sober up and come for supper?"

"Can't. We're here to the bitter end."

"I don't especially like the ring of that."

"Hey. The way I figure it, we, him and me, we can go on indefinitely. We don't need very much and whatever it is I can have it delivered. That's except for those super duper pizzas from Valentino's. You gonna bring them over once in a while?"

"Maybe. I'll think about it."

"If you don't, I'd just have to give up on pizza. Like I said yesterday. Eat one of theirs and you're spoiled forever."

"Want to know something? I simply do not understand your sealing yourself up in that house. The logic of it completely eludes me."

"Okay... It goes like this. Soon as I drive on out of here, that's what starts up most of the serious checking business. I get myself into big time, I mean real, real, heavy concern for being sure of just about everything I do. It can be in the line of my work or something as simple as how I park the damned car on the street. For instance, did I leave enough space in front of it, behind it, to the side? Did I really put enough coins in the parking meter? And when I go back to look at the meter, once isn't usually enough to do it for me. I'll go back and check that fucking meter two, three, four times. And meanwhile I'm starin', bloody wide eyed starin' through the car windows at the little pushbuttons inside, making sure they're down so I know the car's really locked up tight. 'Know'? For me the word has no meaning. I don't ever really get to know, or let's say feel, that's better, feel I know anything, anything at all.

"And lest I forget it, while I'm goin' through all of this, I'm also pullin' on the door handles to make triple, quadruple, as many times as it has to be for me, sure, or as close to sure as a guy like me can be, that the damned car doors are really locked. And when it's the new Ford I'm drivin', when I pull on those handles the inside lights go on. God forbid they shouldn't go off again. That the computer chip or the timer should be defective and the lights might stay on, and the battery run down, and I won't be able to start the car when I get back to it. That's if I ever do get to tear myself away from the fucker. So I stand there and wait the full minute or two until the inside lights go off again. And finally I get to take off. That is unless I'm feelin' real uneasy and have to go through the whole damned thing, or maybe one part of it, a few more times. And that's only what happens when I run the car. Want to hear some more?"

"*No!*"

"You get it now? If I stay right here I can avoid most of that shit. Those cars are where they need to be, in the garage and the garage doors are down. And not only are the garage doors down. A little while ago I went below into the cellar and turned off the circuit breakers for those doors. They're electrically operated. And I turned those breakers off lots and lots of times. So I probably did it right. So no way. No way are they ever goin' up again. There's no juice for runnin' them anymore. That's unless the Horla pulls off some kind of a miracle. Hittin' those doors where they hurt gets me to feeling better. Lots better. Just a little thing like that."

"You call that little?"

"Like they say: 'Whatever grabs you.'"

"But if you pass on almost everything you would ordinarily do, how can you ever manage to overcome your problem?"

"Good question. I'm starting to believe that if all I do is hang in here and limit myself to dealing with the very few things around here that I might still incline to check on, you saw some of them last night, I'll be able to concentrate my efforts to break away. Also, I'll get to confront the Horla, here, on my turf, and maybe on my terms. I'll be the one to call all the shots and he can't pull any new tricks on me, which he can, and easily, once he's got me on the outside."

"I wish you'd stop with this Horla thing. It gives me the heebie-jeebies."

"I can't see how my facing up to reality should be giving you the jitters."

Just a little bit of Adam was going a long way to putting Miranda off.

"Now you listen to me Adam. If in the twenty-first century, facing down a... a Horla is your idea of facing up to reality, maybe you'd better go and have a long talk with your... What's his name?"

"Rogoff? No, I'm quits with him also."

"Great. That's mind bogglingly great. All you've got now is that dumb dog of yours, right?"

"He's not so dumb. And you forgetting my pizza lady?"

"Meaning me?"

"Why not?"

"Not, because I'm not about to buy into some kind of a folie a deux, plus like I said, dumb dog situation. Life is complicated enough. I do not need to get myself involved with a guy who's cute enough but also setting to drive both himself and everyone around him absolutely bonkers. Maybe I should call your Doctor Rogoff and bring him up to date on his favorite patient."

"Not on your life. He's out. Completely out of the picture."

"Then me too."

"Aw come on. Come on now, Miranda. Try and be a good sport about it. What I've also been thinking is this. Rogoff said Prozac has what's called a half life of around a week. That means that in just about the same amount of time it'll be well on out of my system and I can be back to normal with what's important to us. So if by the time it gives with the half life, I'm still at least half alive, we can tie it on again. Before then, it'd be too hard on me, if you get what I mean. Hard on me? Get it? A good one, no? And I'd only wind up being terribly frustrated again."

"Bye bye, Adam. And if you're listening, bye bye, Savage."

No point in calling her right back. Probably, he hoped, once she'd thought it all over, she'd come around. He leaned back and polished off the rest of the scotch.

Well it was time for lunch. Lunch for both of them. Adam put down another sixteen ounce helping of lamb and rice dog food for Savage and warmed the leftover pizza in the microwave for himself. They both ate with relish although no doubt about it, the pizza had been much better as originally served, when relatively fresh from the oven. But it was good to see Savage going for rations more fitting for him than people food.

Later, after sending Savage outside for awhile so he could tend to his business and also chase a couple of cats who'd made the almost fatal mistake of thinking they could interlope on territory now well spotted out and considered sacred to him, Adam decided that the drink and all of this turmoil had taken much of the steam out of him. He was too tired to carry on. Leading Savage upstairs they headed for an afternoon nap. But this time, woe to any intruder. The alarm was set and his no nonsense dog was right there next to the bed.

It was five o'clock when the phone, his only remaining link with the outside, summoned him again.

"Adam. I'm getting ready to leave the office."

It was Rogoff.

"Well fancy that. Whatcha want? Congratulations for a day of professional dedication? You need escort to the bank, maybe, while you stash away you're ill gotten gains? Or if you're waitin' for me to come by or it's some kind of an apology you're after, forget it. Take off. Whatever I said, I meant. This is one politico who means what he says and says what he means."

"You about through?"

"You can say that again. Like I also told Reynolds. Just send me an up-to-date bill. From here on out, that's how I am, out and on my own."

"That's what we need to talk about, the problem we've had relating to one another. I've never believed we had a transference that worked. There's always been too much resistance on your part. Even outright hostility."

"Hey man. It took all these years for you to realize that? Or was the pay too good to resist? And if you supposed that all along, wasn't it downright unethical to lead me on? Have me thinkin' that eventually I'd get something out of it? Christ. The last time it was me who had to break it off. I bet you'd have gone on like forever. Anything to keep your damned meter runnin'."

Rogoff was determined to stick to his guns. He was used to laboring in Adam's line of fire.

"I think you should see another psychiatrist."

"Forget it. I'm through with all you guys."

"How about a woman psychiatrist?"

"None of them, either. Man, woman, you're all the same. You've all been drinkin' too long from the same well. Besides which, the only woman I want, thanks to you, may have just about given up on me. But I'm prayin' she hasn't."

"Adam, you cannot tackle this thing on your own. And I'm fearful you're becoming totally alienated from reality."

"Hey. You haven't even got an exact idea as to what my 'thing' like you call it, really amounts to. One minute it's how I grew up. The next, it's the deep parts of my brain all of a sudden gone kaput. Then I'm not makin' enough serotonin. It goes on and on. You guys make it up as you go along. And as for being alienated, it's not from reality. Reality is right here in my house with my new dog, and where I plan to address my needs and figure out my problem on my own. I'm tight, real tight, with reality. How in hell, anyway, does a guy like you come off to pretendin' he's got an exclusive handle on reality? Who do you think you are? Socrates? Einstein? Confucius? Old Heidegger? Hell. Last I heard, those smart asses couldn't even come near to determinin' what reality was all about. And for my money, you come on more like Fu Manchu than any philosopher I ever read."

"You're refusing further professional help?"

"Help is what you call what I've been gettin'?"

"Whatever you want to call it, you want no more of it. Correct?"

"That's a fair statement. Want me to sign something to that effect?"

"No. I'll just send you a confirmation of our present understanding and make a note in your chart."

"Coverin' your ass, hey? Don't worry. I'm not plannin' to do myself in. And I'm not gonna sue you either. Take care, you old faker you."

This time, it was Adam who had the satisfaction of hanging up.

Twelve

The broadside at Rogoff had been delivered from a position of bedded recumbency. During it, Savage had made no move from his mat. But it was time now, in their tacitly arrived at understanding to live in strict tandem, for both of them to head for the bathroom. Adam got seated on the commode. Savage sprawled alongside him, muzzle pressed to the floor between extended forelimbs.

Adam took, once more, to regarding a reflected image of himself, this time one provided by a shaving mirror set upon the marble sinktop directly before him.

"You," he considered, "are one sorry sight. But aren't you? And now you've gone and given up your crutch. There'll be no more Doctor Rogoff to lean on or to fight with."

But what was left for Rogoff or other doctors of his ilk to offer him? Once analytical talk therapy was given up on and drugs had been counted out, there would be nothing but supportive kinds of urgings to be more accommodating, to knuckle down, accept, give in and go along like other, the more reasonable people. There'd be unending, insufferable, pleadings that he toe the necessary, the conventional line, and make the most of what time there still remained to him. He'd be pressed to forego his resentments, his remorse, his regrets over missed opportunities and wrong or foolish choices he'd made in the past.

And above all, he'd need to stop reaching in everything, for perfection. Its attainment would always elude him and the failed quest for it must inevitably floor him emotionally and exaggerate his tendency to check. His checking, by such a theoretical linkage, could be explained at least in part and perhaps be reduced if only he accepted how foolish it was to pursue perfection. How many times, on their first go 'round, had he had to endure that kind of mumbo jumbo from Rogoff? Astonishing, how easy it had become now to recall all of that old time psychological double talk. No wonder he'd repressed those previous overreaching pronouncements before returning to Rogoff's office this second time.

At the age of forty-six, of course there had to be certain expected limitations, even terminal kinds, requiring dumb surrender. Cancer perhaps? An obscure infection with no known cure? An accident like an auto collision or a plane crash? Okay, he'd go along with such dicey happenstance. He could face up to it. Accept it.

But this? Concede away everything except respiration? Recognize he had no recourse but to go lockstep with those already brainwashed and overmedicated? Spend the rest of his life, a god damned puppet? And someone (or something) else would work his strings?

Once he gave up like that he'd have to be thinking at least forty percent or more of the time. "Hey. I don't want to do this. It's altogether unnecessary. It's even fucking crazy." Yet have no recourse but to comply. And to observe that his resentful acquiescence brought no security. So what if with other final agonies there could be pain or physical failing or in the end, even a coma? With his present lousy deal the very essence of being, of having real substance, was going by the board. Unless he did something and got about it very soon, he'd never again be his own man.

It was right. He was right. To choose otherwise. Better to hide out, to hole up with a single companion, his dog and thereby preclude all those extraneous circumstances in which his will could be preempted. Perhaps, if he could win only a few minor skirmishes with the Horla, here, on home ground, there'd come a time when he could break out for a wider engagement of this usurper of his will and of his mind.

His will? The way things had been going, it was hard to pretend, he still had such a thing. Its only vestige, was this oddball but determined connivance to somehow thwart an ignoble and fractured end.

Adam headed back downstairs, Savage charging before him. He turned off the alarm system and allowed the dog a half hour to himself in the backyard while he took an early dinner consisting of the same scrambled eggs, ham, toast and coffee he'd had for breakfast. Then Savage was brought back inside. Man and dog took seated positions in the den and regarded one another.

"Well? What's next? Where do we go from here?"

Savage responded by swatting Adam's knee with a front paw, sharply scraping his long curved nails into it.

"Hey. That doesn't help any. More pain isn't what I need. And don't tear the pants."

This time the chastised dog accepted his reprimand

without retaliating and squatted before him, at first appearing pensive, but soon his eyelids drooped and he was asleep once more. Although seeming to be quite out of it, his ears responded to any outside sound by elevating and pivoting in the appropriate direction. Asleep or not, this animal was no doubt making uncanny judgments as to the nature and the propriety of everything Adam could hear and then some.

Before settling down in the den Adam had already begun to consider a new but tentative plan of action. It was conceived over eggs upon taking his first nibble of toast. So to ask Savage for his opinion had not been intended as a really honest overture. But he was getting into the habit, now, of sharing almost every thought with his dog and to air it, occasionally, as a question. Savage had just decided, without ever opening an eye, to growl at something beyond human kinds of earshot. As soon as his rumbling quieted down, as part of this new approach, Adam began to think aloud.

"Okay... I've decided that although you are primarily here to ward off human kinds of evildoers, you can help me with another sort of favor. I've decided that we're gonna pick up where I left off with Reynolds. But this time out, you and I are gonna do it alone. And since nothing, absolutely nothing, seems to faze you, maybe if just a little of your certainty about everything and your downright doggedness, so to speak, could rub off on me, even a little, I'd be considerably ahead of the game.

"Also, you get yourself good and ready because we are not going to single out some solitary maneuver for verification avoidance. You and I are going, all at once, to tackle just about everything around here, except for those

God damned garage doors. And we are not even going to give ourselves the chance to think, did we or did we not check something out properly. We're gonna be too fucking busy rushing onto our next challenge to worry about what we did with the last one. Get it? We're gonna take on so much and all at once, it'd be a miracle if we could even remember very much of what we'd just been into. And what we can't remember, can't bug us any. Right? But listen up. I'm really counting on you to see me through all of this. To inspire me with your kind of assuredness. Okay?"

Savage responded with manifest exuberance as Adam arose and with quickening pace headed for the stairs. Soon his new master was hurrying along, often taking two steps at a time until arriving slightly winded at the third floor level. As fast as Adam's ascent had been, he was no match for the dog. Savage fairly flew up the stairs, always staying at least a step or two ahead of Adam, and periodically turning back in wide mouthed panting excitement to see if Adam was managing to keep up with him.

The third floor consisted of two finished rooms which had never been lived in. The entire area, which also included a bathroom and several walk-in closets, had fallen into disuse as a storage area. Old clothing, old books, nonfunctional furniture, were scattered about and set in haphazard teetering piles the site of which was always disconcerting to a tidy person like Adam.

Even though this part of the house was infrequently visited, just to think about its chaotically dispersed contents, always gave him bad feelings and yet he never took steps to sort through its contents, trash what was no longer needed, and store away the rest, neatly. It was as if he had to preserve the privilege of visiting this topsy-turvy hideaway or remember the slipshod surroundings as an occasion for some kind of essential self immolation. The fact that this upper region of the house was removed from any significant possibility of daily sighting made no difference. He knew full well that the mere existence of a place like this was cause for a simmering rancor regardless of whether or not he chose to stop and think about it.

Although they harbored, at best, only inconsequential memorabilia, whenever Adam did visit these rooms, particularly since the re-advent of the Horla, he included as many carefully conducted maneuvers to assure the security of this part of his house as he did any other. But today his purpose was to hurriedly undo all of those previously executed safeguards by sweeping through the place as quickly as possible and hastily re-secure it. He must not pause to repeat anything. He must not allow himself the time to even second think the accuracy, the validity, of any particular, even trivial maneuver.

He climbed up and unlatched a window, then refastened it. Rushing into the bathroom, he opened all of the water taps and retightened them, but only once, not twice, not three times. Each and every light switch was moved to an on position, then set to off. Closets were opened, then closed. Radiators were turned full on and then full off.

Savage and he, without so much as a glance behind them, raced down to the second floor. There, each of four rooms were entered. Television sets were turned on, then off. All of the windows were opened and closed. Radiators again, four of them, on and off. Auxiliary heaters were plugged in, turned on, turned off, plugged out. Taps in two bathrooms were opened and closed.

Following that, Savage, joyously and all out committed

to the frantic pace of this mad dashing about, anticipated him and scampered before him to the ground floor where Adam unlatched every door to the outside then proceeded to lock each of them again. Finally, he lunged into the living room, turned on lights, television, audio components, flicked them off once more, dropped into an armchair and looked down at a completely delighted, open mouthed, panting dog.

One could not imagine a more pleased and worked up Doberman. Nor might one encounter a more despairing human being. It hadn't worked.

Aside from that wrenching realization, Adam knew that this had been no mere imperfectly executed, but still promising false start. He was now gripped by so much anxiety that he was absolutely sure that his hastily conceived method could never fly. Worse, he'd suffered a bitterly sensed setback. Rather than being empowered to comfortably forego any reflection upon the details of his pell-mell antics, or being barred from individual recollection of them by virtue of their sheer numbers, he could do nothing but agonize and strain for their complete recall.

Adam was obliged to concern himself not only about what it was he could remember but even more so about what he couldn't call to mind. He may have disturbed an essential, required order of things in his house by virtue of his hasty passage through it.

And so he had no option but to make his way back upstairs, to drag pitifully and reluctantly upward, all the way back to the third floor, and to labor there for some measure of reassurance that what he'd thought to be secured was actually fastened, closed, tightened, or otherwise attended to properly. Savage appeared to mirror Adam's heavy mood. This time around, he lagged behind Adam on the stairs, barely brushing occasionally against his master's heels as Adam trudged upwards. The dog clearly wanted no part of this tedious replay. For Savage, as well as for Adam, it was a senseless charade. But Adam, the more highly evolved creature, was stuck with it.

It took him a full hour to do what had to be done on the third floor alone. All told, more than two hours elapsed before Adam could work his way back down to ground level and collapse into his chair in the den. And still he wondered, had his retreat been executed properly? What might have been overlooked?

As Rogoff had stipulated, some obscure sense of a true and final closure was denied him. Ultimately, only exasperation, mental and physical fatigue, the embarrassment of so much overkill, and his suspicion that even much more could not possibly suffice to abort his excesses had brought him to a halt. Pathetically, this stoppage of his was no more than a state of restive, dissatisfied, still questioning uncertainty.

It was now pushing ten o'clock and the still of his house made this kind of existence all the more oppressive. Should he turn to television? Try to lose himself in triviality or in what had no bearing at all on his condition? What point to it? Nothing to be gained and probably something to be lost in mindless diversion. That would be wasting of his precious time. After all, there was an elusive and ponderous reality waiting to be faced up to and made sense of.

He gave his thoughts free range. How, conceivably, could the Horla be part of anything even touched by reality? Christ. He had no faith in a god so how might there exist some other kind of spirit, and a malevolent one to boot, lurking about, and haunting him? If God made no sense, how could a Horla? Or did the Horla represent guilt and self punishment for his impugning God's existence over the years. Or rather was this the way God meted out *His* kind of retaliatory retribution? But just to think like that implied a certain shallowness to his oft-stated atheism.

To Adam, as an unhappy adolescent, the Horla constituted punishment of mysterious origin, for doing something he shouldn't be doing. After all, there was all that clandestine and guilt-ridden jerking off. Now, thirty odd years later, here was the upshot of all that Freudian *sturm und drang* and taboo. Here sat a bedeviled grown man, medically certified to have some kind of a critical biological fault, and forced to confront not only new and esoteric psychopharmacological questions but also the same old unapproachable ethers.

Well, at least the dog at his feet had undeniable substance. He prodded him with a toe.

"Hey man. Want to watch the evening news?"

He was promptly rewarded with a growl reminding him once again that Savage did not suffer those foolish enough to make hostile gestures.

"Okay, okay. No television. We'll read the paper."

The New York Times, resting on the footstool before him, was his only habitual daily. He could easily skip past the front page. Its content was as remote to any personal interest he might have as anything he'd be likely to encounter on television. New horror stories from Afghanistan had displaced the political high jinks he wanted to read about to the back pages. And their grim accounts were becoming especially too tedious to bear with on a daily basis. Anyway, those Middle-Eastern fools had made their own beds. So let them damned well lie in them. Enough was enough. Tonight especially, he had no patience for any more of those bleeding heart stories that the overpaid foreign correspondents were putting out every day. He had his own troubles to think about. So Adam skipped to the financial section and strangely enough here was quite another thing entirely, a fascinating article. He, or rather his kind, had made it into print. Soon what he'd read had him thinking furiously. He deliberated uninterruptedly until the phone summoned him away.

"Hello, you've reached 362..."

"Cut it out, Adam. I know it's you. And I have questions, not messages."

"Miranda. Great to hear your sweet voice. It's like from heaven above. But tonight, and no put down intended, any voice represents a welcome tiding. That's how low this boy has fallen. So what's with the questions?"

"You've answered them. I see you're feeling much better than before."

"Yeah, well Savage and I ran sort of an experiment that didn't turn out too cool. In fact not only was it a bust but it had us, or me at least, in one helluva funk. I'd say, of the two of us, he came out not too badly. You want the grim details?"

"Not especially, but I know by now that when you have to unload, you have to unload."

Adam proceeded to describe his evening of despair.

"...and fiasco or not, it may have represented my very last creative thought on how to beat this rap, at least independently."

Miranda was even more appalled than previously. "By

running up and down the stairs with Savage nipping at your heels?"

"Where'd you get that idea? He hasn't bitten anyone, yet."

"Wishful thinking. Maybe a nasty bite would bring you to your senses, make you go for help. There has to be somebody out there with ideas on how to treat this."

"Forget it. We've run every possible program. Unless you want me to try voodoo, acupuncture, or something else totally stupid, we are, you might say, dead, real dead in the so called therapeutic waters."

"You have a way with words, you know that? Real cheery kinda words."

"Well I'm not sure where Savage and I are headed from here on in but now I know that at least we're not alone. In fact, we made the papers."

"Okay... I give up. Clue me in."

"Just before you buzzed me I came across this story in the *Times* financial section on what is called burdensome behavior. It's really all about people who can't control their spending. That's the connection with big bucks issues. But the writer also does a pretty good job of looking at compulsive trends in general. He hits on alcohol, gambling, drugs, food, as well as on people who can't keep themselves from overdoing the shopping bit."

"So? When you do you intend to come to the point, if ever?"

Adam knew he'd better reach it posthaste or this girl was going to hang up on him again. Hard though. The Horla, or whatever, required that he be vigilant, touching each and every base.

"The *point* is that this here article establishes me. It does it independent of what Rogoff and Reynolds have told me. And what's more, all at once, I've got this incredible feeling I'm not alone out there. Or in here, for that matter."

"How's that?"

"By the numbers gal. By the unbelievable numbers. As sort of a casual inclusion in this freaking article they print a table, a table of figures. And you know what?"

"No, I don't know *what*. How could I, you fool. I didn't read today's Times."

"Sorry darling. You're right. Anyway, the table shows that 2.1 percent of the population is just like me."

"You want to bet?'

"Okay... I'll yield on that. It's simply that the population is 2.1 per cent obsessive-compulsive. So in this country alone, I don't know about worldwide, that means there are more than four million of us obsessive-compulsives. How does that grab you?"

Nothing was coming from the other end so he resumed.

"We obsessive-compulsives constitute a down to earth significant minority. We could be a lobbying group, a political force, a voting block. This is stuff I really know a lot about. Heavy stuff. We don't have to be shut-ins, homebound. We can start demanding action, a bail out. And you wanna know something else? People like us don't give up. We never give up. It's not in our nature to give up. We just keep doin' what we have to do over and over, and over and over and over and over... "

"Stop it. Stop it!"

"And over and over again. All we need is to get together and to get our act together. We gotta organize, mobilize."

Miranda could sense that Adam, heretofore a person of somewhat deliberate and paced manner, his ways being understandable and in keeping with either his gloominess or his compulsivity, was now on the verge of becoming all-out maniacal. Hers was a considerable dilemma. By posing further questions to him she might very well provoke some kind of a declarative explosion. And to question in any way what she anticipated and secretly feared was going to be his logical and quite obvious next step couldn't possibly deter him anyway. So she'd be respectfully mum. He'd certainly need no suggestion from her to persevere. As he'd said, it came natural to guys like him. Adam was on a fearsome roll.

"Gotcha dumbfounded hey? Yessiree babe. Now hear this. First step and in keeping with the time tested fact of there being mucho strength in numbers, we, that is you and I, my sweet little advertising know it all, are gonna run us an ad in the paper to announce the formation of a brand new society, the O.C.D. Society International. Get it? That's short for obsessive-compulsive disorder. We will start us a membership drive. And maybe tomorrow I'll even design some kind of a logo. Christ. We will have officers, our own stationery, and guess what else?"

She allowed herself what seemed a safe question.

"What?"

"As soon as we get responses, then comes the pitch for annual dues. We will offer everything from corresponding membership to associate to senior to even lifetime arrangements. I'm willing to bet you, lifetime is gonna be our most popular option. Makes sense, doesn't it? Took us a whole lifetime to get into this mess. Why not devote a lifetime to bustin' out? And then, once everybody's signed up and procedural matters are defined and structured, we can even offer some kind of an official status to family members. God knows. Over the years, they've probably suffered every bit as much as we sickies ourselves. What do you think we oughta call that kind of membership?"

"How about Family?"

"Brilliant. Downright brilliant. Why didn't I think of that?"

"They also serve who come up with the best ideas."

"Touché."

No doubt about it, she thought. At this loony moment in time 'teched' was the right word for him and just about the whole situation.

"Adam? I'm awfully tired again. Why don't we talk about all of this tomorrow?"

"No problem. Savage and I have our work cut out for us tonight, anyway. We gotta draft organizational announcements for both the Times and the Post so that we're ready for the weekend editions. That way there'll be nationwide, even some international coverage. Also, I need to set up a separate phone line and voicemail for the society right here at the house. Got to keep my other numbers free for personal business. I know this is all coming at you kind of fast and furious but that's always been my professional style. Hit 'em fast and hit 'em hard. That's my way. The only way. Damn it. Until the Horla got it into his evil mind to circle back and waylay me, nobody out there, just nobody, could get the jump on me.

"But what you have to understand is that this is not about misery lookin' for company. Do not for a moment get that idea. Far from it. There's a bottom line to all of this and that's not it. It's to take all the money we're gonna collect, dough I'm countin' on to come pourin' in. First thing tomorrow too, if I should forget, remind me. We gotta apply real fast for tax exempt status. Because we need to take every last red cent, all of that dough, and fund us some real down to earth or for that matter far out sophisticated research, if that's what it takes, whatever flies, happens to work best, and get to the bottom of all this shit.

"There's gonna be no more goddammed Freudian put downs. Or behavioral bullshit. No more sellin' us two dollar a hit capsules of Prozac. We don't need to trade off our manhood, or our womanhood either. Or go on flights of silly fancy. Or have inappropriate highs. Or stumble around not even knowin' what day it is. Let those self servin' drug companies go belly up that are tryin' to sell us on chemical pie in the sky. To hell with them for settin' to hook us on a lifetime habit that'll really blow our ever lovin' minds. And for what? For makin' it possible for some drug company CEOs to get even richer than they already are? Richer on poor slobs like us. Slobs stuck on a god dammed treadmill. Blood money is what they're out for. Blood money for blood suckers. Goddamnit. That's what that amounts to.

"And for Christ sake, don't anyone dare mention, we do not want to hear as much as a whisper about someone settin' us up for psychosurgery. I'm willing to bet there are surgical creeps out there just waitin', droolin', over maybe gettin' the chance to pull off something like that. They better lay their damned scalpels and their cauteries down. We will not put up with it. We are holding on to the deep parts of our brains. And we're not gonna take it anymore. No way. We 2.1 percent are organizin' and settin' us up an action group."

"Tomorrow, Adam. Let's leave it until tomorrow."

Again, his newfound friend was gone. But what did he mean by "anymore"?

About a week had passed since he'd been back to Rog-off and received the doctor's first detailed and presumably well-informed medical opinion regarding his so-called disorder. But his determination to indulge in self-exploration, exaggerated by so much isolation, had soon caused him to cast about in what seemed the primordial world of his first privileged breaths. Oh but it had appeared to be such a promising world. He could just about see himself there, starting out like all the rest. He had experimented, groped, fumbled. It was all so indiscriminate.

Until mysteriously it had kicked in. The ancient gift of automatism had taken over and by a kind of destiny, it became incorporated into his antics. Then, ever so briefly he could be freewheeling, casual, and was able to romp like all the others, making free and joyous use of this wondrous gift. But then came the first inkling of something going wrong. It had turned on him, taken him over. There'd been a fault, somehow, in his sampling of that ancient offering.

From then on, from time to time, and finally, maybe even permanently, that ages old biological device for automatic repetition would run him, not he it, and having no reasonable prospects for governing it, he was confronted with more and more of its demands.

Now he strained for remembrance of what it was like when briefly he'd been free, both way back then and for awhile later on, during his up beat so-called "times of remission." Yes. The Lord giveth and the Lord taketh away. So blessed is the name of this Lord?

He'd just see what his action group had to say about that.

Thirteen

The following evening Miranda telephoned Rogoff.
"Doctor?"

"Yes? Who's this?"

"Look. You don't know me. But I'm a friend of Adam's."

"Miracle of the ages! He's got a friend? Sorry! I shouldn't have said that. Anything wrong? He's not in trouble, is he?"

Miranda had expected to be asking all the questions. And now, if it was she who'd have to come up with all the answers, no doubt about it, Adam was going to stay in trouble. Deep trouble. Nevertheless she'd start up again. Her need to know was urgent and concerned the depth of Adam's plight, not its mere substantiation.

"Do you think he could be, or get like..."

"Psychotic?"

"Right. That's the word."

"Can't tell you."

"Why not?"

"First off, you are not family or otherwise privileged by him to have such confidential information. He'd have to give it to you in writing. Second, I do not know what his present mental state might be. Because thirdly, he's no longer my patient. He fired me! Want any more reasons?"

"Now look here, doc! This man has holed himself up with a Doberman Pinscher and two guns for some kind of a last ditch stand in case anybody should try and break in on him. Also, he is setting, may even have already done it, to run ads in newspapers calling for membership in what he calls his International O.C.D. Society. And the last word from him was he wasn't going to take it any more!"

"Christ! The son of a bitch!"

"That's it? The Lord's name in vain and a curse? For *that* you went to medical school and he's been paying you dearly?"

"My God! You sound just like him! I don't need this!"

"Need? What you need? I should think the important thing is not what you need but what *he* needs and right now. Pronto!"

"I really don't know what to say."

"A psychiatrist who doesn't know what to say. That should be one for the books."

"You sure you two aren't related?"

Miranda saw she'd have to take a different tack with Adam's only--present or past--doctor.

"Look, doc! Mark my word! Whether or not he knows it, I represent what may turn out to be Adam's very last plea for help. Now just suppose he goes through the window or blows himself away with one of those shotguns he's sleeping with. Or in some kind of a fool rage kicks that new dog of his just a little too hard. So if it comes out, and I'm telling you it will, that at this critical moment you turned a deaf ear... Well let's put it this way. Your insurance coverage real good? All paid up, is it?"

"Look..."

"Miranda's okay."

"Look, Miranda, I'd like to be helpful."

"Now we're getting somewhere."

"But I'm in a very difficult position."

"Let's just focus on Adam's position."

"That's what I'm trying to do. You see, even if he were still my patient, I'd have to say that what's going to happen is utterly unpredictable. For all I know, though it's very unlikely, this exacerbation of his obsessive-compulsiveness may just blow over. And there's no way anyone can force him to resume the usual things we ordinarily recommend. He's tried them all and he wants no part of them.

"As to whether or not he's on the edge of a psychotic episode? How am I to fathom that? I haven't seen him for days now and there's not much chance I will. But from what you've told me, I wouldn't think so. After all, Adam has always been very imaginative in his approach to just about everything. And militant too! It's his stock in trade, you know. Workwise, so to speak. And from the little you've described I can't see that he's a threat to himself. To some burglar? That would be another story! He sure resents that break in! But that is a police, or a legal matter, not a medical question. By the way are those guns of his registered?"

"How would I know that?"

"Well, being as orderly and compulsive as he is, I think it's a safe bet that they are. And if you think, from what you've described, there are grounds for marching in there and committing him, forget it. No chance! Although his may be a very narrow and odd reality, he's quite in touch with it. And when you think about it, what's so unreasonable about creating an O.C.D. Society?. There are all kinds of organizations of a medical nature set up by laymen: Alzheimer's, M.S., Parkinson, to name but a few. Maybe he'd even take comfort from hanging out with other sufferers of the same disorder. Now can I ask you a personal question?"

"Sure."

"How long do you know this guy?"

"A little over a week."

"And you..."

"Like him, I like him a lot. He's kind of sweet."

"Well... anytime you feel the need. Don't hesitate. You come and see me."

"What the hell is that supposed to mean?"

"You don't have to get defensive."

"What's to be defensive about?"

"I simply thought that..."

"You want to know something, doc? There's no need for you to sweat this anymore. Adam's dead right. You stand to be of no help at all. No help whatsoever. And you want to know another thing? I'm from the old school. The school that thinks it's wrong, awfully wrong, when doctors try to proposition people, especially healthy ones with normal concerns, into being their patients. Look it up in a book, doc! You'll find it under 'concern normal.' So don't count on hearing from me again. You have yourself a real nice evening. And if you don't happen to know it, it's illegal to tape record a conversation without first getting the other party's permission. So turn off your damned machine! Adam's right about that too. You seem more interested in protecting your rear end than in exploring his troubled mind."

Well what had she learned? Nothing at all. She'd have to form her own judgment about Adam. Rogoff had spewed no more than generalities. There was only her common sense to lead her.

She hastened to call him. He responded, it seemed, almost before the first ring. That made her feel, however unrealistically, that he could as easily have been listening in on her conversation with Rogoff.

"Adam speaking."

"Good. I hate leaving messages. How's Savage doing?"

"Well right now he's resting. We've had a busy day."

"Really?"

"Right. We've got the extra phone line in already. No sitting around on a waiting list for us! I happened to remember this guy I know with the phone company. Nothing like a little pull to make the wheels go 'round."

"Should I bring another pizza?"

"I'm tempted, but we'd better not. It was too damned frustrating for me the last time. Know what I mean?"

"I suppose so but I can only take your word for it."

"Let's just wait until I'm off the Prozac another couple of days. Okay? Besides which we've got our work cut out for us. You got a fax machine over there?"

"Yes. Sure."

She surmised what was coming. By now it was easy to anticipate him. Once this ultimate compulsive, had decided on something, there was no stopping him. He was predictably relentless.

"Okay... I've drafted the ad. I'll fax it over to you and you come up with however it needs changing. Then we fax it to the newspapers and we're on our way. Exciting, no?"

"You bet."

This was awful. She was reduced to humoring him. It must go no further. He'd read her. Which he did.

"Aw c'mon Miranda! I haven't flipped and don't intend to. You haven't been boning up on people like me, have you? Well, whatcha find out? Spill it! What do the books say about us? Do we change into were-wolves or something when people aren't nice to us? Or do we just go more seriously bonkers?"

"Listen Adam. Like I've already told you. I'm a very busy lady. I don't have the time to go hunting down any medical libraries. You want to learn about yourself? You go there!"

"Well Okay... Give me your fax number."

In a few minutes his ad was transmitted and they were back on line again with one another. She was not just a little incredulous.

"You really want to send this thing?"

"Something's wrong with it?"

"Come on Adam! What's with this? 'O.C.D.ers of the world arise'? You crazy?"

"That's the general idea, kiddo!"

"Can you really see *The New York Times* running a pitch like this? Not on your life! There's no way! They'll take it as a call for some kind of revolution."

"What's so wrong about that? Just as long as it isn't an armed one or against the government, it should be cool enough. Listen. I'm dead certain it's within my first amendment rights."

"Well look at it another way. How about the people who are supposed to respond to this thing? If you have it sounding belligerent or downright silly they are going to ignore it. I run ads all the time! Publicity is about being appealing, not confrontational. And most of the poor men and women who have what you have are probably either terribly embarrassed or in the closet about it. Right?"

"Well... I suppose. Okay, tidy it up so it'll move and fax it back to me later tonight. I gotta submit it first thing in the morning. And say! You were supposed to remind me about that tax exempt status thing and you didn't! Why'd you screw up like that?"

"Sorry, Adam. Today was a shambles at the office."

"That's all right. Savage and I remembered anyway. We've got a call out to a legal guy who deals in things like that. And meanwhile I'm drafting the articles of incorporation. We'll just model it after something I did years ago. Would you believe it? A tax exempt deal for fixing up, get this, the private home of the Governor of the Virgin Islands so that someday, after he had passed, it would be like a shrine to the bastard's memory! The egotistical jerk had already nailed his name on every public building he could get hold of. And the tax free money we came up with? Christ! He even used it for a new Olympic-sized swimming pool, a sauna, and a five car garage. How do you like them apples?"

"Well if you could put a deal like that together, I suppose there'll be no stopping you with a simple thing like O.C.D. International."

"Leave out the 'International' bit. I've already decided on that. First, we better see how it works out over here. I forgot that once you start reaching out worldwide you open yourself up to all kinds of problems with other country's internal codes and regulations and a whole different set of bureaucracies. You also need to get yourself expensive translating services which in the beginning we may not be able to afford. Let's just skip all that. At least for now."

"You've a wonderful mind, Adam. You know that?"

"Now don't you mock me!"

"I'm not! This other business, the compulsive stuff, I can see clear through all of it and to the real Adam. I firmly believe that you're clever, and gentle, and you've got a terrific sense of humor!"

"Yeah, yeah. I'm the cat's meow! But ain't I though? That's why I'm locked in, alone, like in solitary, with nasty boy here, and trying to come up with some kind of a breakout! That's why my old lady took off too. Not because we drifted apart, mind you. It was the drifting together with a neat guy like me that spelled curtains for us!"

"You tell me not to mock you and then you wind up putting yourself down. You shouldn't do that. It can't be good for you."

"Okay... We'll just tend to business. Before you turn in tonight, fax me back what I'm gonna need tomorrow."

"Yes sir!"

Only remotely, however much he liked her, did he entertain thoughts of an enduring relationship with this bright and energetic gal. Because, say what she would about his mind, he knew otherwise. It had been laid low, maybe even mortally, by the Horla. Psychiatrists and neurologists could call his problem whatever they wanted. And they could lose themselves in jargon over Meshugeh behavior, and genes, and serotonin, and brain cell nuclei, and chemical imbalances, and deeply placed brain cells in what they called a caudate mucleus, crapping out, but in the end, for all their well informed pretenses, they couldn't come up with anything in the least bit useful to him. On the other hand, he could. For he'd found an adversary, a thing to engage, to take on. The Horla! And all of his energy had to be conserved for what, most certainly, had to come.

Fourteen

Very late that same night, Miranda returned by fax a considerably toned down and revised version of Adam's outreach to fellow O.C.D. sufferers. It was sparse, tasteful, and eye catching. In line with his suggestion, return mailings were simply to be directed to the Secretary-Treasurer of the O.C.D. Society. The address given for the organization was Adam's own and the telephone number was the new one. There was promise of a monthly newsletter and request for an initial up front fee of a mere five dollars. Actual enrollments would cost more, depending upon categories of membership. It sounded very reasonable, especially since he was convinced there were at least four million people out there having only other very expensive and quite useless options.

The following morning, after a pretty good sleep, induced possibly by the taking of three milligrams of melatonin, he transmitted the ads to *The New York Times* and *The Washington Post* by fax and by phone charging them off to his VISA card. Then, after receiving assurance from a lawyer friend that to secure tax exempt status would pose no problem at all, and with freshly drawn articles of incorporation in hand, as modified from his Virgin Island enterprise, he felt privileged to sit back, rather pleased with himself, and await the consequence of what he'd set in motion.

The fact that he'd slept well was probably a sign that the Prozac was well on its way to being leeched from his system. Until now, as pharmacologically described, it had made it difficult for him to doze off at night and had occasioned his need for the afternoon naps he'd started taking. If not for that first one, he'd probably not even have slept through the damned burglary!

As for the melatonin, he placed little credence on much touted claims it could induce sleep. He had decided to try it because a month ago he'd spotted something on the cover of a book in his neighborhood health food store, waxing elegantly of its effectiveness. There was a subtitle conveying to the product a "miracle" status. There was no way that Adam believed he could afford to pass up on a miracle. Particularly one that went for only twelve ninety-five, required no F.D.A. approval, and was being panned by most of the medical profession. More than enough to highly recommend it.

A miracle. For certain, a very interesting circumstance, if one could call an outworldly thing a circumstance. But Adam, in a way, was now somewhat out of this world, or in between worlds, and might that not be where miracles were most apt to take their special kind of form and be encountered? Bumping into or arranging for such a thing couldn't be all that bad. Now could it?

Every once in awhile his business phone would ring. He had an extension of it at the house. And someone would want to start up new business with him, or ask why he wasn't in his office, or try, like the fellow who had caught up with him and Miranda on the street, to hold him to some kind of prior commitment. He ducked and dodged and prevaricated or outright refused to do anything but stay rooted where he was. Stay rooted and wait for that which had to be awaited.

Several days passed. Days in which he continued to chat with Miranda by phone, his ever more bonded dog at his feet, and taking in every word of it. These were also days during which he began to grow a beard, ate an awful lot of Chinese food delivered to his door, and waited for responses to his ad. He was trying to do as little checking as possible, but there was some anyway. Maybe it had even increased a little. In any event, it remained unbearable.

Finally, four days after the ad had run, he got a call.

"Hey! This O.C.D. Anonymous?"

It was a man sounding a bit pressed and maybe also misguided.

"You've got the right place if you leave off the 'anonymous' part. We do not intend to hide our identities around here. We are dead set on coming out."

"Yeah? Well what 's with the ad? And what do I stand to get if I send you my fiver?"

"We're going to fund new research on O.C.D. Try to get it started at some leading university. The idea is to circumvent the vested interest of the drug companies and the old boy network of psychiatrists. And there'll be newsletters, symposia, conferences, annual meetings."

As he made his pitch, Adam was becoming more and more charged up. But not the guy on the other end.

"All for five bucks? You gotta be kiddin'!"

"Hey man! You know there are four million of us? Figure it out for yourself. Do five times four million and see what you come up with."

Soon it didn't look like Adam had a taker, numbers or no numbers.

"Sounds like a come-on to me. Or maybe a scam. You could be just fixin' to line your own pockets."

Adam was desperate to enroll his very first member.

"Look. Drop us a line. As soon as we have our membership forms printed up we'll send you one and we are prepared to offer you a lifetime free membership as a founding member. How's that grab you?"

"It doesn't! Now I really smell a rat!"

"Where?"

"Where? I dunno where! I only smell it. I don't see it!"

"Well, what else can we tell you to change your mind?"

"Okay... You a washer? Me, I spend all day washing my hands. Hell! There are times I wear the damned skin offa' them! And the medicine don't help me none."

"Precisely. The medicines now available do not stand to cure anyone."

"Answer the fucking question! Are you a washer or aren't you?"

"No. I'm a checker."

"A checker? A fucking low down checker! And you are gonna presume to tell me how to run my life? What the hell does a checker know about it? About what it means to be a washer?"

"It's all the same thing. It's all about being compulsive."

"Says who? You just told me we first need to get the research done."

The man had a point.

"Look... "

"I ain't lookin' and I ain't spendin' and I ain't joinin' nothin' either! Fuck off, buddy!"

He was gone. Not a very propitious start for his national membership drive. Well, at least the ad was being picked up on.

Another two days passed. And during them he spent an inordinate amount of time searching for a variety of things. Things like his army discharge papers, his high school and college diplomas, and particularly the official instruction booklets commonly packaged with newly purchased mechanical and electronic devices like the lawn mower, the dishwasher, his cellular telephones, the audio equipment, the tape recorders. It seemed there was no foreseeable limit to the number of such documents that had been set aside somewhere over the years and that now he was peculiarly constrained to rummage about and search for.

Unfortunately, he had not the slightest need for any of them. He had no problem in operating or in servicing a single one of these items. It was just that his mind, having not much else to occupy it, and being by odd chance crossed by the recollection of some such device and happening next to wonder where the instructions for it might have wound up, became ambushed. Soon his mind became inalterably waylayed by a veritable cascade of intense concerns regarding the whereabouts of the printed instructions for just about every device he owned. And it was not to be satisfied except by immediate, appropriate, retrievals.

But once their recovery was accomplished, then began a series of protracted revisits of the sites selected for securing such newly found booklets of instruction in order for him to be dead certain they were really well retained in their new locations and that he remembered exactly where they now happened to be.

What was becoming of his theory that by withdrawing from the world at large he'd be able to limit his compulsively motivated activities?

The day after this lamentable and purposeless quest had begun he received a second call on his ad.

"Sir?"

It sounded like a young woman.

"You know what it's like, don't you?"

If Adam didn't, no one did. But he quibbled.

"Well now, that depends. The symptoms do vary from case to case."

"Well I can't help myself. I keep having these evil thoughts. And they're always about men and you know what? You can probably guess at what I'm going through. You can, can't you?"

"Look. I'm no psychiatrist but I suppose you're subject to what they call obsessional thinking."

"Could you tell me something"

"About the society we're proposing?"

"No."

"Then what?"

"Why, the color of your eyes, silly man! They're brown. Now they are, aren't they?"

Adam felt constrained to clarify a few things.

"Madam. This is about joining the O.C.D. Society. Not a dating organization."

"Well you sure could have fooled me!"

Then the woman started to giggle, and Adam thought he could also hear a couple of men laughing. In fact he was becoming sure that all of this was being listened to over multiple extension phones at the other end.

"This some kinda gag?"

"Come on now! Blow us a little kiss and we'll get to feeling ever so much better!"

Then the laughter was definitely audible. A lot of it.

"You want I should also go into my heavy breathing routine? You goddammed buncha perverts!"

One of the men came on.

"No, no, dearie! All we want is a lovely little kiss!"

"Fuck off!"

Now, in addition to all his other worries, he had a further concern. Would nuts like these, once they had the number, start calling back for no reason other than to bug him? Who could have anticipated such a thing?

But there was no quick call back.

Still, an hour later, when his O.C.D. phone rang once more, fearing for the worst, he ripped through his announcement a tad curtly.

"O.C.D. Society!"

This time it was a very nice sounding young man. And at once, officiously apologetic.

"Have I reached you at a bad time?"

What other kind of time did Adam have? But he lied.

"Not at all."

"Would you mind telling me about your organization?"

Adam did just that. As completely as he could. He gave it his all. The whole kit and caboodle. His entire rationale along with his hopes for the future of O.C.D. as he envisaged it. The more he went on, the more innervating his rundown became for him. Finally he had to wrap it up. It was really getting to him and he didn't want to sound overly excited.

"Well that's simply marvelous! My name is Scott. I represent the *Broadway Weekly* and we are prepared to run your ad on a weekly basis at a very nominal rate for a three month period. Think you might be interested?"

"Screw you!"

These three calls were all he would receive in response to his advertisement in the two newspapers.

However disappointed Adam might be for all of his manifestly wide of the mark assumptions regarding the eagerness on the part of O.C.D. sufferers to join up and close ranks with him, Savage was entirely unaffected. In fact, the dog on man bonding process had firmed up so well that in all likelihood, he would have turned resentfully jealous had Adam's venture succeeded. Savage was not the kind of animal attuned to sharing or to patiently vying for attention. Apparently, he'd never spent enough one on one time with a human being before to warrant the conviction he had come into full fledged ownership of one. But now he had Adam all to himself.

It was probably a lucky thing for Adam that such a creature was prepared to offer him this unlimited degree of close company. It was only his backyard excursions of necessity with the dog and his venting of resentment for what life had dealt him, that provided Adam with any distraction at all from his unrelenting compulsive behavior. Here on his home grounds, to his consternation, that nefarious habitude had mushroomed to a level never realized when he was still moving about in other places. And yet there was not the least temptation for him to abandon what had become the ultimate torture chamber. Holing up in this old house had become irreversibly fixed to his other undeniable obsessive urges.

If there were any saving thoughts that conjured up the possibility of escape from his agonizingly monotonous inclination to check on everything under the sun, it was the conviction that now the Horla was right there, full-time, and in a state of vulnerable permanent residence.

It had to be. What other reason was there for him being so much worse? And so it was coming down to himself, Savage, and the Horla. Now the three of them would see it through to a finish! Often he stared at his ever present dog and wondered if Savage might be the one to finally nail the fucker!

Fifteen

It was a week later. He'd become sullen, was losing track of time, and solidly rooted in his tedious waiting game. At around 6 PM, there was a heavy pounding at the front door. Looking through a small barred window he saw that it was Miranda. Prompt admission was conceded by him and his dog. Savage could now be counted on to distinguish good guys from bad, even assuming an admiring stance with a certain Chinese delivery man from a nearby Cantonese carry-out, in line with his conveyance of particularly appealing aromas.

As for Miranda, Savage seemed not to peg her as serious competition for his and Adam's relationship. The dog was quite capable of such sophisticated distinctions. So upon Miranda's entry, he fell to wagging the remains of his tightly cropped Doberman tail rather exuberantly.

For days, Miranda had been commiserating with Adam by phone over the collapse of his O.C.D. project. And now, burgeoning with high English cheer, and loaded down with care packages drawn from a local gourmet market, she was poised to escalate her efforts. But to Adam's mind she was being inappropriately effervescent.

"What yuh so happy about?"

Miranda was not deterred. "Why after all these days... the mere sight of you, old darling! And guess what? I'm intending to grill for us these two specially aged Old Angus New York strip steaks. So, then do these ears of mine get to hear 'Bravo, Bravo' or don't they?"

Adam turned to Savage. "Whatcha think? Interested?"

Savage's stump wagged enthusiastically, maybe even ecstatically. But then he started to squirrel his nose into two packages Miranda had rested on Adam's front hall table, where she'd thought to be safely setting them down, at once she recognized her tactical error.

"You! Sir Dog! Cease and desist! That meat is for the pleasure and sustenance of people, and not for four legged creatures, not even a huggy-cuddly one like you. However, if you are a real patient little dear, and behave yourself accordingly, we'll save you the scraps."

Turning to the other member of this well knit pair, she bubbled on. "Well then! At the very least, do I get a nice little peck on the forehead? Remember? Something like that which you planted there at the Kennedy Center eons ago. Which was when I started to think you might not be such a bad sort after all."

Adam obliged her. Woodenly at best, but he got the job done.

"How's that grab you?"

"Marvelously so! Have you been practicing?"

"Only on Savage. C'mon now, Miranda. Knock it off. Lightheartedness doesn't cut it around here."

"Very well then. That little kiss of yours? For all I got

out of it, it could just as well have been bestowed upon a corpse in her casket! Is that what you'd rather hear?"

"Right on! A spade's a spade! No point in tryin' to duck reality. Especially the kind we've got around here."

"Brrrr! The devil you say! Permit me to enlighten you on that very issue. Because tonight, we had very well better! Her ladyship is determined to take the place over and put a light and airy cast on this little old funny farm of yours, at the price of that nasty old so-called reality. Let there be no more of the gloom and doom gambit you're so headily into. So now then! Do I get invited out of this imprisoning front hall, or don't I? Unless you've cause to object, I'd like to make for the kitchen."

"I'm sorry. Sure. Let's head on outa here. And how about a drink?"

"I thought you'd never ask. Very well, when you pour your scotch, make mine a gin. And please? Just a little ice, if you will."

Adam was never one for uncertainties.

"Okay... So there's gonna be steaks an' drinks. What's the game plan, otherwise?"

"Otherwise? Could I be hearing right? Look here Adam! By my calendar, that Prozac of yours has been well gone now for quite a while. By every logic, and not much intuition, it's about time for us to resume close to where we left off. Any chance of your remembering that?"

"How could I forget? It was awful. But now we're destined to make it all better."

"What makes you so sure?"

"The Horla went and told me!"

"Hey! Around here, we don't joke about him."

"Very well. I sincerely apologize. And let me make it

up to you. For example, would you like to feel my boobs? Either one will do quite nicely."

"We better wait 'til later. Right now I'm kinda leery a' testin' those particular waters. Know what I mean? Let's just proceed with the cookin'."

"All right. Slow and steady is how we'll take it. Like they say, `by your pleasure, my lord'."

Miranda and Savage were half way to the kitchen when she happened to stop with an afterthought.

"And why'd you not answer your phone today? I must have called a dozen times."

"That's a good question."

"What's a good answer?"

"I couldn't think a' anythin' worth sayin'. This here situation is hopeless. I'm flat out a' options and gettin' worse by the minute. Take this mornin' for instance. When I brought Savage back in from the yard and we had the outside door locked behind us, I felt compelled to go back on out again anyway. So we did it. And more than once. We did it over and over again.

"You wanna know why? Not to be sure I'd locked the gate to the yard. No! It was to see if by some crazy chance, and when I say crazy, I really mean crazy, I'd left Savage outside. In spite of him, all along, bein' right there beside me! Ain't that fuckin' pathetic? My dog's right next to me watchin' all a' this shit and probably tryin' to figure out what the hell I'm up to. Christ! I was knowin' all along he was damned sure there, and not still outside, but I went through this sick routine anyhow. Hey! I went and did it half a dozen times! So why would I want to spill all a' that over the phone and just wind up upsettin' you? Anyway, I knew who it was from your number comin' up on my I.D. pad each time the phone rang. But I sure didn't think you needed an earful a' my nutty goin's on to make your day."

"It would not have bothered me in the least. It was much more upsetting to get no answer. For all I knew, something monstrous might have happened."

"Guess what, kiddo? It has! He's here full time now. An' just chippin' away at me. So don't you go baitin' him any, like you were a minute ago!"

"Always... that precious Horla of yours. It's absolute and utter nonsense. But we shall simply put him out of mind. There now! Where might your griddle be?"

They'd been heading towards the kitchen during this on and off exchange. Once there, he pointed to what she needed hanging from a hook above the stove. While he got started on the drinks Miranda continued to bubble away, ignoring his bleakness.

"What a splendid griddle. And just look at these steaks!"

None of this could mitigate his grim rootedness.

"You wanna know what really pisses me off?"

"Pray tell... but immediately. I don't enjoy guessing games. Especially with you. I'd only be striking out. So rave on, if you must."

"It's the fact that no one joined up with me. And I don't believe it's because we didn't have enough ad coverage. There's just too many of us out there. Lots of O.C.D.ers must have caught that ad. And it has nothing to do with costs of membership. What the hell does five bucks amount to? Especially for people who buy pricey weekend editions of the the *New York Times* or the *Washington Post*. No. It's that the poor sick bastards are just like me. They're done an' gone for. They're irreversible. And they damned well know it! So why, I ask you, should they add to their woes by comin' on out'a the closet?"

They were sipping their drinks now, he at the kitchen table, Miranda hovering the cast iron griddle upon which her inch and a half steaks were crackling and throwing off quite a bit of smoke. Cooking seemed to further her natural liveliness.

"I ask you, but doesn't that smell great? And we've got cole slaw and apple pie to boot. We shall be having ourselves a veritable ball! Chocolate ice cream too. But tell me, if you would, why does this particular gin taste the best ever?"

"It's Bombay gin. Like English, and maybe originally, only for Rahjahs. But what the hell do I know about gin? Anyway, you haven't been listenin'. Haven't been payin' any attention to me at all."

"You're wrong! I most certainly have! I just don't see why any of that should make you mad at those poor people. So what if they caught the ad but couldn't bring themselves to reach out? I'd have thought that you, of all people, would simply wind up feeling sorry for them and utterly sympathetic."

"Hell! I'm not mad at them! It's the situation we're all up against that's got me ticked off! Except for the one crazy guy, that washer creep, no one even tried reachin' out. Until all a' this happened I'd never have dreamed what a sad fix our two per cent of the population was really in! Don't you see that, Miranda? More than four million people, by there very silence, are signallin' somethin' awful! They are sayin', without sayin' anythin' at all, that they've damned well given up! And forced to doin' exactly what I'm stuck with doin'. Just livin' with the fuckin' thing as best they can. You see, none of us are ever gonna be like you, a normal kinda person. Because people like us are all born different from you and your kind. And me? I'm even gonna die different. I'm sure not ever gonna be like old Lorin Maazel! When my genetic dice got tossed, I struck out. That's why I'm not normal. And why I'm no super-duper musical prodigy, either! Everything. It's all been spelled out. Past, present, and the future! And there's also this other thing, the Horla, makin' damned sure of it, once you're slated to be a real goner! So if you've got any sense you'll drink your drink, have your steak, and all the other little goodies you've so generously fetched us, and clear on outa' here. I'm expectin' only a bitter end, which is what we are imminently waitin' on. And it's not gonna be worth the watchin' for an upbeat kinda gal like you."

Miranda closed the distance between them, looked him straight in the eye and winked.

"How do you prefer your steak?"

"Rare."

"Very well then. Go set the table and we shall get on with it! Because our steaks are nearly ready!"

The food was as good as promised. And far better than the Chinese or other neighborhood sendouts he'd been subsisting on. The drinks, the meal, the company... who could reasonably want anything better? If he could only keep this up, what actually was there to go outside for? It was sheer whimsy but inspired him to reiterate his earlier pleading.

"It seems like only yesterday I was describing what a neat setup we three could have here. No?"

"I remember when it was only us two."

"Well if you don't think this here dog is willin' to buy

into the deal, you just toss him the end of that steak and set yourself for big time adoration! I tell you though, you are one helluva cook!"

"Don't try buttering me up, Adam! Though I must admit, I do cook fairly well. It's just that all I did tonight was char a little meat. And if those steaks were any rarer than I served them they might have galloped right on out of here!"

"Hey girl! That's weird!"

"You see? You are not the only abnormal one around here!"

"Yeah. Thank God we've got old Savage here to keep us honest, and on a reasonably even keel. So what's next?"

"Desert?"

"Not for me, thanks. I'm plain stuffed."

"Right you are. So then... while you're putting Savage out, I'll just pop our dishes into the machine. Then by the time you're back inside, having checked on whatever needs checking, I'll be all tidied up, in bed, and ready to roll. What do you think of that?"

He seemed strapped for an answer.

"Hey! I asked if it was okay?"

"A little while ago, I was thinkin' to myself, `who could ask for anything more?'"

"I'll take that as a yes."

Savage dashed outside and relieved himself so hastily, Adam half wondered if he might be thinking himself the one so artfully invited upstairs. He was certainly more hyped up than usual. More likely though, he'd picked up on Adam's excitement and was merely reflecting it. But however enticing Adam's immediate amorous prospects might be, any impetus for entering into a loving engagement with

Miranda hardly precluded what needed to be run through before being freed up sufficiently to join her.

And now, out of concern that a night of inordinate passion might induce him to be careless in the execution of a much earlier than usual set of lockup procedures, a lot more than the customary amount of checking was required.

It took him and Savage nearly a full hour to get the job done. Or at least done well enough for him to finally lumber upstairs. Except that he was forced to accommodate the inevitable, the predictable urge to go back down again, this time without Savage who had by now given up on him. He stared wide-eyed for quite a while at the security panel arguing himself into the suspicion that there existed a significant likelihood he'd previously armed it correctly. When finally he arrived in the bedroom, both Miranda and Savage were dead to the world. Savage didn't even stir as he undressed, turned off the light, and slipped under the covers.

Miranda came awake on being touched. "Everything locked up?"

"How the hell would I know?"

"It's reassuring to hear you say yes and so sweetly."

"Listen up. I been wonderin' while downstairs."

"Heavens! Why? And what!"

"Well you know... it's like everythin' else. Once I start thinkin', I can't just stop."

"Now this is really getting to be ridiculous. Can't we forget all that and make love?"

"Sure, sure. But first I've got these questions for you. You mind, huh?"

"Yes, you fool. Of course I mind! But very well, out

with them, and real fast! I'm not sure how much more of this I can take."

"And you'll level with me?"

"Adam, how many times do I have to tell you? I never lie."

"Okay then. Here we go. Now since we were together last... anybody else?"

"My God! I can't believe this is happening! You have anyone in mind by whom I might have, shall we say, become tainted?"

"Look, I don't take any chances.

"The answer is no. Come on now, Adam. Try and relax, and let's get something going here."

He had a go at it and so did she, but it was no use. It was even worse than last time. Then, at least, there'd been full arousal. And now, not a thing was happening. Nothing at all.

Miranda was nice enough. Diplomatic too.

"All right there sweetie. Let's just go to sleep. We'll live and fight and possibly make love, some other day."

Although she proceeded to sleep, Adam lay awake for a long time, listening to the sounds of her breathing. Depressed, dismayed, he worried his way through the new problem. Could he really be that unfortunate? Unfortunate enough to be the kinda guy that just a few doses of Prozac could wipe out so completely? It took a few hours but he got to sleep also.

Sixteen

Well, but not for long.

At first he thought it just one of those frequent times at night when Savage would growl softly during a dream or on hearing something outside beyond ordinary human range. But that was not the case. The dog had sounded off, minimally at first, causing Adam to stir. But now it was a very loud, sustained barking, and the scrambling, scraping, sound of a dog's hell-bent charging feet which suddenly brought Adam, chest pounding, bolt upright in bed. Miranda was also awake and calling out.

"What's that?"

By then the dog was far below and somewhere toward the rear of the house alternately snarling or barking furiously. Also there were other sounds, sounds of voices and scuffling feet.

Why in hell hadn't he realized it? Was his hearing blocked or something? One of the voices was female and coming from his alarm system. It was screaming "Intruder! Intruder! Intruder! Sensor 18!"

Adam hastened to break some very disquieting news to Miranda.

"It's the back door! It's been forced, that's what! And he or it is gonna' fucking well be here for keeps this time around!"

Adam switched on a light, grabbed for his pants and took hold of his shotgun. As usual he had it on the ready, beside his bed. It hadn't been moved since the first break-in.

"Oh my God Adam! Don't be crazy! You can't be going to use that thing. Call the cops! And leave it to Savage until they get here. Please! Please! Please!"

Adam had no time for argument.

"Can't use it? Shit! Whatcha think I did in 'Nam? Listen up, woman. Get under the bed! The alarm's already out to the cops. It's automatic but Savage doesn't know that and it'll take time before they get here. So there's none to spare. Besides which, no god damned creepy bastard's gonna harm a hair on his head. Not so long as I'm around. Now move it! Get under the damned bed!"

Adam turned off the light again. With his 12-gauge held at ready he descended the stairs. Savage was no longer barking. Then, after moving cautiously through the den and dining room, he learned quickly that Savage was still very much alive. Because from the direction of the rear door, situated at the back of the kitchen, he could hear, not further barking but a very mean and ominous sounding, throaty rumble. Otherwise, and also definite, a sort of heavy breathing.

He moved further forward and began to crouch. Next, he slipped the safety. That was when he noticed how marvelous he felt. He'd bolted from bed. He'd unhesitatingly issued Miranda's orders. And now he would have to face up to what could be a very dicey situation. Noting that he'd slipped the safety without even a second thought, he was astounded by his absolute certitude of there being no possibility he'd wasted even a moment to check and see if he'd done it properly.

Hot dog! This was it! It at last! This was how one lived, really lived, Goddamn it!

As he came nearer to the back door and his eyes became better dark adapted he could see that it had been forced open. And there was the evildoer! He was young and light skinned, standing in a corner of the closeby hallway, just opposite the violated door with his back pressed against the wall as tightly as he could manage it. Savage stood before him growling, upper lip curled back, front teeth well bared and menacing.

By now the alarm had stopped sounding. It was supposed to do that and to reset, thirty seconds following activation.

So far, the intruder was not aware of Adam's presence. Adam doubted he was even armed or by now he'd surely have taken a shot at Savage. So it ought to be relatively simple to just let Savage have his way and keep the guy exactly where he was until the cops arrived. He'd not even bother letting on, before then, that he was there and eyeing all of this. He'd let his faithful dog enjoy himself.

Suddenly, however, the guy began to call for help in the direction of the open door across from him.

"Pete! Fer Christ sake! Where the fuck are you?"

Damn it! There had to be an outside man! A lookout or someone to assist in making off with what they'd intended to snatch.

"Pete! Get in here and shoot this fucking dog before he grabs me!"

Adam could feel a squeezing or twisting sensation deep in his upper abdomen as he overheard movements outside the forced doorway. In another moment, Savage, still in place, was barking furiously again. Then, the figure of the second burglar appeared. Adam could make out an arm, and a hand holding what surely had to be a gun.

Oh what a tremendous roar it was! Adam was quite familiar with how shotguns sounded. He'd fired them in open fields. But he'd never opened up with one indoors and in so confined a space. And the pungent smell of exploded gunpowder was equally overpowering. It seemed also, under these conditions, to have a pleasant taste to it.

By now the second man was screaming unintelligibly. Adam had shattered the fellow's right arm with a well aimed round that also sent his revolver flying off somewhere into the darkness beyond the doorway. He could hear sounds of the man apparently falling across the steps leading up into the outer hall and backyard.

The first guy pleaded with him.

"Mister! Please! We give up! Call off the damned dog!"

Adam would have none of it.

"Why? Why should I? That's what he's here for. He's gonna keep you company while I go out and see to the other Horla!"

It wasn't incomprehensible that the cornered one failed to make out what was happening.

"The what? You crazy, mister?"

"Right! I'm crazy! Everybody knows it. Everybody says it. And for the first time, I love it. I really love it! I'm relishing every damned minute of it! And I'm gonna be sorry when it's over."

Stepping past the cornered figure and patting Savage

on the head as he passed him by, Adam went through
the open doorway. The second man was sprawled across
some back hall steps a few feet away. Although the light
reflecting from outside was limited, he could discern that
this one was quite a bit older, somewhat burly, darker
skinned, maybe Spanish. And he was not taking any of
this very kindly. He alternated moans with fearful screams.

"You son of a bitch! You blew my arm away! And for
what? A fuckin' mutt?"

"Watch your mouth, buddy! To me, that dog's like my
own flesh and blood!"

"Yeah? Well I'll be back and when I am, I'm gonna
cut the two of you!"

Adam pivoted slightly to flip a switch for the back hall
ceiling light. Now he could make out the revolver. It had
fallen to the concrete and was well beyond the reach of felon
number two's left hand. As Adam turned again to face him
the man reached with that hand to a side jacket pocket for
what Adam, a sometimes reasonable person, anticipated to
be a handkerchief for binding up his bloodied right arm.

But the guy had gone for something else. It was a
long pearly knife handle, sheathing no doubt, an equally
long sticker. Suddenly the guy managed to press down
upon the handle's spring release and to snap the very
nasty business end of the knife from out the handle. In
no time at all he was lunging desperately in Adam's
direction and yelling.

"I'm gonna carve you up right now, you mother fucking bastard!"

Adam moved quickly to one side leaving the fellow
to thrust at empty air. The man had to be deranged to be
lunging at him like that. At someone still pointing a shotgun.

Particularly someone not recently all that level headed and whose gun still held another three rounds. Also, what this would be burglar couldn't possibly grasp was that this someone could now be all too easily provoked into externalizing a dreadful amount of pent up resentment and rage. And directing it at what he might imagine was most hateful to him. Rogoff would have been glad to so inform him. But Rogoff was home in bed. He wasn't there, in the back hall.

"Yeah? Well Okay, Mr. Horla! Here's what I think of your knife!"

Adam fired the remaining three rounds. At close range. Each being directed into one of the unfortunate man's still intact limbs. He was stunned by the calamitous din. The thunderous blast of the gun, Savage's ever louder barking and snarling, the screams and howling curses of the men, the overwhelming eye-smarting pungency of gunshot exploded at such close range, taken separately or together, they were far more than enough to finally render him immobile and unthinking. For the moment he felt free. Free of both body and mind.

Then there were outside voices.

"What in all hell is going on here!"

The police, responding finally to the alarm system, were coming in past the door to the yard, it also having been forced by the intruders. Savage continued to bark. Only the intruders responded to the cop's question.

"We're being murdered that's what!" Screamed the one still cornered by Savage. The other, the four times wounded one, was now reduced to god awful groans and sobbing.

There were two uniformed officers plus two in plain clothes. It was one of the plainclothes men, apparently a detective, who took Adam's gun from him. By now Adam appeared trancelike and was barely grasping his weapon, pointed limply downward in the direction of his own feet. The detective shouted at him.

"Mister! Call off the damned dog!"

No response from Adam.

Then there was an intervening voice from somewhere inside. It sounded a little plaintive and yet managed to enjoin. And maybe also, it floated before it some kind of an appealing fragrance. A fragrance that was subtle but still strong enough to compete with the smell of all that gunpowder.

"Good boy, Savage! Now you come on back inside with me! That's a sweet little doggie. Come on now, love!"

The sound of Miranda's voice called Adam back to what could only be an unwelcome awareness. He saw that she had leashed his wondrous canine and was drawing him back inside. And now there'd be bothersome declarations and queries from these policemen.

"Hey Mike! Call an ambulance! This one's really torn up bad. Christ! There's blood all over the place. And cuff the other one before he tries somethin' cute. Mister! You with it yet?"

Adam turned toward the detective and spoke.

"Hey, I remember you! You were here last time and suggested I get myself a Doberman. That was terrific advice. You know that? And, boy, am I grateful to you!"

The cop remembered full well.

"Right mister. But I sure didn't advise anything about semiautomatic shotguns or trying to exterminate someone once you had him down! Even if it was one of these miserable buggers!"

Then the detective posed just a few questions.

"You got a license for that gun?"

"No. Brought it back from 'Nam."

"And is that where you thought you were tonight? Had what they call a flashback?"

"Nope. The bastard was gonna come in here and kill my dog. I was not about to stand for something like that! He had a gun. Then a knife. So I made damned sure he'd never try it again, anywhere. That's because aside from Miranda, that dog is all I've got."

"But you had him in both arms. Why the legs too?"

"I don't know how to answer that. There was something else involved, but I don't know exactly what it was. Right now, it escapes me."

The detective was far from satisfied.

"Uh huh. Well this is all a little too fuzzy for me. And the gun's not registered either. I think, after the ambulance gets here, you better come along with us to the stationhouse. I'm gonna have to leave it all for the captain to try and sort out."

Miranda had returned to Adam's side.

"What's up, Adam?"

"I gotta go with the police and see the captain. How's Savage doin'?"

"Fine. I gave him biscuits and closed him in the bedroom."

"How about callin' up the guys who did the repairs when I was broken into last time? I wrote their number down on the cover of the phone book. And could you stay right here until I get back?"

"Sure, Adam."

Seventeen

Adam didn't come back. The captain thought better of releasing him, convinced he was much too strange to be running around loose, especially in his precinct. Besides which, the shooting, however provoked, was done with an unregistered, illegal weapon which spelled trouble for anyone in the District of Columbia. Moreover, there was an almost gangland air of calculated mayhem to the whole business because of the methodical way by which he'd dealt with his home invaders.

So Adam found himself under arrest awaiting not only psychiatric evaluation but also further police investigation. Hearing what lay in store for him, he exercised the privilege of calling Miranda. She found him in the city jail to which he'd been transferred for preliminary processing prior to formal lockup.

At ten o'clock the next morning she arrived at his holding area and was directed to a room secured for visitations. Two armed guards led him in.

The sight of Adam in orange prison garb was a shocker. "Adam! This is outrageous!"

"What's your problem? The color doesn't become me?"

"Okay! Stop the kidding! When's your lawyer going to get you out of here? You know... make bail or do whatever they do."

"I don't want a lawyer. Not even a public defender."

"Are you crazy?"

"Yes! For the umpteenth time! Why can't you manage to understand something so obvious? All the guys around here know I'm flat out nuts. And two shrinks also. So why can't you?"

Miranda wasn't buying. She persisted in believing he was just kidding around. That idea changed quite abruptly. Leaning forward over the table between them, Adam took her into a softly spoken but firmly expressed confidence.

"Look'a here babe. I've been doin' lots of heavy thinkin' since they grabbed me. Or maybe it actually started up when I was back there at the house, in the rear hallway, right after the shootout when I was in kinda' like a daze. So here's the thing. Let's face it. I'm a lost cause, kiddo. And I'm never gonna be any better. Especially if I stay on the outside where the Horla can keep getting at me.

"So what I've decided is that as long as I'm here, he fucking well can't! Do you follow me? What I'm saying is that where I am right now, there's not a damned thing for me to check on. In here, there's absolutely nothing that belongs to me and whatever little I need, all of it, is provided. And not only that, but around this place, it's someone else who's got to do all the locking up. And the double checking, too. You see what I'm driving at? This is a much better deal than the mind crippling drugs or all that behavioral therapy bullshit. It's the first time, really, that I've gotten the monkey off my back. Damned but if gettin' jailed hasn't turned out to be a godsend. That's what it is, pure and simple. A fucking godsend!"

To say that Miranda was incredulous would be a gross understatement.

"This is wild. Wild! Wild! Wild!"

"You'll take care of Savage, won't you?"

"What about us? You and me?"

Adam was a well-tested professional. To work every conceivable angle had always been his special calling. This would be no exception.

"I don't know if you've ever heard about it, but I got it straight from the horse's mouth. There's a guy in here who's done lots of time. And what he says is that there's a thing called conjugal visits. How about that? Neat! Hey?"